the el

SLOTH

VII

UINCENDUM NATUS

GIANA DARLING

lust

pride

wrath

envy

gluttony

sloth

greed

Sloth
The Elite Seven. Book Six.

Copyright © 2019 Giana Darling
Edited by Word Nerd Editing
Cover Design by K Webster
Photo from Adobe Stock
Formatting by Stacey at Champagne Book Design

To Ker Dukey, K Webster, M.N. Forgy, Claire C. Riley, and J.D. Hollyfield.
Thank you for your sisterhood while we created our fictional brotherhood.

"No man deserves to be praised for his goodness, who has it not in his power to be wicked. Goodness without that power is generally nothing more than sloth, or an impotence of will."—Francois de La Rochefoucauld

Warning: this book is not for the devout. It's a tale of blasphemy, sin, and murder. If you can't handle scenes of sex in a church, villainous religious figures, and burning holy objects, this book is not for you.

The Elite Seven Character List

The Deadly Sinners

Lust—Rhett Masters
Pride—Mason Blackwell
Wrath—Samuel Gunnar
Envy—Sebastian Westbrook
Gluttony—Baxter Goddard V 'God'
Sloth—Rush Dempsey
Greed—Micah Dixon

The Holy Virtues

Chastity Griffin—Dean George Griffin's daughter, Lillian's step-daughter, and Rhett's girlfriend

Megan Thorne—theology professor at St. Augustine's, George Griffin's niece, and Mason's girlfriend.

Patience Noelle—Mayor's daughter and Sam's girlfriend

Sabella Gunnar—Sam's twin sister and Sebastian's love interest

Zemira Coleman—God's girlfriend

Isabelle Savoie—Archbishop Savoie's daughter and Rush's girlfriend

The Elite

Lillian Benedict—St. Augustine's guidance counsellor, Dean George Griffin's wife, Malcom Benedict's sister

Baxter Goddard IV 'Four'—God's father, third richest man in the world, and one of the top leaders of The Elite

Malcom Benedict—Lillian's brother and one of the top leaders of The Elite

Archbishop Savoie—the catholic head of St. Augustine's Cathedral and Isabelle's father

Ward Dempsey—Rush's father, Louisiana's state senator, and one of the leaders of The Elite

Mayor Noelle—Patience's father and the mayor of New Orleans

UINCENDUM NATUS

PREFACE

the elite seven

Since 1942, The Elite Seven Society have created and guided influential leaders, molding the country into something better. This society was birthed by Malcom Benedict, II who wanted more for Americans. More wealth. More influence. More power. Some leaders have the skills, but not the influence, and that simply wasn't fair according to Mr. Benedict. He invested his own money and time to construct a society that bred the best of the best, year after year.

But to be the best, you must be ruthless.

Good leaders make sacrifices. Sometimes the sacrifices are hard, but the rewards are plentiful. Mr. Benedict made sure to indulge these leaders with their utmost desires.

A devout Catholic himself, he designed a society that rewarded his leaders with the sins that were frowned upon. If they were giving up love and happiness and joy for the betterment of the country, they deserved something in its stead.

Pride, Envy, Wrath, Sloth, Greed, Gluttony, and Lust.

Choosing leaders for this society means that it takes intense focus. Only seven are to be selected, and the investments and time are showered upon the new seven chosen every four years. The predecessors of each group of seven choose people who fit the sin that will mold them into who they are needed to be in the future—what America needs them to be. This is after a detailed study of many potential candidates. The university's acting dean behaves as a liaison for the society bringing the college applicants to the predecessors so that the selection may begin. The society members who are going out will bring forth a candidate that the society votes on and approves.

After they are chosen, the initiates are given a token and an invitation to initiation. The initiation will be a test to their character and ability to do what's right for the betterment of the society. Once the initiates pass their test, they are discreetly branded with the mark of the society, and are groomed through challenges during the course of their elite education to breed them into the influential people they were meant to be.

Once in The Elite Seven, there is no getting out. The money and power are their reward. Should they choose to stray or break the rules, the society strips them of everything. Anything they once had will be removed.

Opportunities will never arise. They will no longer have the support of the society. To this day, there have been no known occurrences of anyone from the society having to be banished. This elite group of people are what every young man and woman aspire to be a part of. While the group is a secret society, they are whispered about amongst the privileged folks in the country. Anyone who is anyone knows of the group and secretly hopes it's their son or daughter who are selected, for good fortune is showered on the family for decades to come.

SLOTH

VII

UINCENDUM NATUS

VII

UINCENDUM NATUS

ONE

Rush

They were fighting again.

Only…it was difficult to call it a true argument when my father stayed mostly silent and my mother rallied against him in a voice shrill enough to wake the dead. I'd wondered as a child if that was exactly what she was trying to do: raise the unholy spirits lurking in the bayous and cemeteries of New Orleans to rally them against my demonic father. She had taught me about voodoo and the magic of the afterlife since I was young, and even though I knew better as a seventeen-year-old man, there was still a small part of my soul that believed Magnolia Dempsey was magic.

I could hear the yelling through the walls and all three stories of our plantation home tucked away in the lush countryside north of New Orleans on the banks of Lake Pontchartrain. A storm was raging outside, one of the savagely wet and windy tempests that crashed through Louisiana in the late summer and early fall. The howling of the wind was nearly as piercing as my mother's screaming.

Other than our five live-in servants, no one was home.

My brothers had long since fled the nest for warm climates and sunny futures while I was still stuck in the thorny bed of the Dempsey compound.

They could have been fighting about me. They often did. My father thought I was a waste of space, and my mother thought I was God's gift. It was hard to agree with either of them, especially when I'd just been blackmailed by my high school girlfriend with a fucking sex tape. I'd tried to hush the situation by myself, and as a result, she'd uploaded the thing to the internet for everyone to see.

Dad sued her family under child pornography laws, but that act was the final nail in the coffin of his contempt for me.

My mother thought I was the victim of a venomous woman scorned because I couldn't and wouldn't love her.

They were both wrong.

I deserved neither his criticism nor her praise.

I was a fucking pigeon in a murder of ravens, and it had never been more obvious.

I was high as fuck, the bay window beside my bed thrown open to bring the storm into my room and let the sweet smoke of my joint carry into the night. Getting high was about the only thing I was good at, or even cared about these days.

SLOTH

Even then, I wasn't high enough to ignore the shatter of glass on the main floor and the resounding vibration as a door slammed shut. My bloodshot gaze caught a flash of white whipping through the backyard under my window.

My mother was running over the wet grass and discarded magnolia blossoms toward the white capped waters of the lake.

Alarm ripped down my spine like tearing Velcro.

The lake was large enough to be truly frigid and fucking dangerous in this kind of weather. She had no business even being out in the slashing force of the rain, let alone anywhere close to the churning body of water.

I crushed the end of my blunt against the windowsill and clumsily ran down the curving staircase and through the hall to the back door. My father's office door was open, light spilling into the dark house from his stained-glass Tiffany lamps. I spared one molasses' slow moment to blink at his figure sitting ramrod straight and totally composed behind his palatial desk.

There was no sympathy or urgency in his dead gaze, only bone deep disregard for everything around him. His house, his wife, and even his youngest son.

I turned back down the hall, sprinting into the plummeting rainfall. The grass was slick and cool as an ice rink beneath my bare feet. The darkness of the storm had completely reduced my visibility of the lake.

Still, I ran, knowing my mother was out there somewhere, more hysterical than I'd ever seen her—even through the last few months of her increasing anxiety.

"Mom!" I shouted over the wind and crashing waves. "Mom, get back from the water!"

A forlorn wail met my ears, but I couldn't be sure if it was the savagery of the storm or a cry for help from my mom.

My feet met the cool, gritty sand, and I went dashing across the sliver of shore until I was ankles deep in the sucking, brutal drag of the lake.

I rubbed my fists over my blurry eyes, hating myself for not being sober or capable enough to fix this mess and fucking find her.

"Magnolia!" I shouted so loudly, it tore a strip off the inside of my throat.

A flash of white caught my eye, pulling my gaze to the left. I peered through the gloom to discern the spill of her dark blonde hair and her pale face bobbing, half-submerged in the frigid lake.

Without thinking, I ran into the waves up to my hips and then dove under the glacial water. My arms churned through the peaks and troughs of biting cold until I finally reached the distance I'd seen my mom at, but she wasn't there.

"Magnolia!" I cried hoarsely, my hair whipping into my eyes and my teeth chattering so hard, my voice was barely discernable over the wind.

Vaguely, I was aware of flashlights on the shore near the house.

Help was coming, but I couldn't rely on them.

I had no doubt they would be too late.

"Rush."

I searched frantically for the whisper of my name, but there was nothing in the wind.

"Rush, I can't do this anymore," my mother said again, her voice so weak, it shot terror straight through my heart.

"You can't fucking do this to me," I panicked, more driven to save her than I had been to do anything in my life. "Where are you?"

"Behind you," she said.

I whipped around and spotted her, bobbing like waterlogged driftwood a few yards deeper into the lake. Her head disappeared under a wave, and when she emerged, there was a soft, sad smile on her face.

"I couldn't live with it," she called brokenly, water gurgling from her mouth as she slowly drowned. "They would have killed me anyway, if I told. This is better. For once, my fate is my own."

"Don't *fucking* do this," I called out, slashing through the waves.

The current was too strong, sucking her out even more quickly than I could swim.

My heart pounded so ferociously in my chest, I thought I was having a heart attack even as I pushed myself harder, swallowing salty water, the saline stinging my eyes, arms and legs burning with excursion and skin glazed with frost.

"The Elite," she gasped. "Please, *cher*, stay away from them."

I panted, but a wave took me under before I could take a proper breath and I lost all sense of direction in the frozen currents. When I finally broke through the surface, my heart was thrumming in my ears and my breath rasped too loudly through my throat.

I couldn't hear her.

I held my breath, focusing on the wind and the waves, trying to dig beneath it for her faint, accented gasp.

Nothing.

I swam in circles, calling her name until my arms felt numb and my legs throbbed like open wounds in the salt water.

I didn't find her.

Even the neighbors and servants who arrived to help in boats couldn't find her after they'd dragged me kicking and screaming from the water.

The cops, when they arrived, were important fucks who stared out at the scene of the crime with pursed lips and pitiful eyes. They thought she was crazy for doing what she did, a frantic woman committed to dying.

One look from my father, who stood amid the frenetic scene like some pillar of indominable strength and marble will, settled it in their minds.

Magnolia Ward had gone crazy and committed suicide.

When they found her a week later, when the skies had calmed and they had time to drag the lake for her body, the autopsy proved she'd had too much alcohol and a collection of heavy prescription pills in her system. If the waves hadn't killed her, the toxic concoction would have.

They wouldn't listen to me when I told them what had really killed her.

I was just the fuck up youngest Dempsey kid who'd been stupid enough to get hypothermia trying to save his crazy ass mom.

No, actually, it was more than that.

When I mentioned The Elite, the policemen's faces froze for a moment before reanimating. And my father... he smiled—actually fucking smiled when I accused the enigmatic Elite for killing my mother.

And then, he said the words that formed the backbone of my mission for the next year.

"There is no blaming The Elite or even claiming them unless they want you, Rush. At the rate you're going, I have little faith they will, and if they don't, you'll never have the answers you want. The truth is, your mother was weak, and you got that trait from her. You don't have what it takes to be one of The Elite because you don't act like a true Dempsey. You never will."

UINCENDUM NATUS

TWO

Rush
One year later.

Three things shaped my life in my first nineteen years of existence.

The first—being born a Dempsey—was something everyone else in my family would have called a blessing.

I called it God's joke.

I was born on the day my father first ran for mayor of New Orleans. As a result of my untimely arrival, my mother was forced to miss his announcement speech and his image suffered. People didn't want to see a good looking, single, rich dude talking about creating jobs and improving education in one of the USA's most poorly educated states. If they were going to see Ken, they wanted him outfitted with Barbie, their two-point-two kids, and their dream house.

He lost that first race because of me.

From there on out, I was my prestigious family's biggest disappointment and eternally appointed black sheep.

The second thing was the worst of them. The night before my eighteenth birthday, my mother, Magnolia, was killed.

The police ruled it a suicide, but when the Senator of Louisiana's wife dies under mysterious circumstances, what else are you going to do but cover it up?

Few people knew the truth. Not even I knew the extent of my mom's motivation for drinking herself into oblivion and then swimming out into Lake Pontchartrain during one of New Orleans' worst storms.

The only thing I knew for sure was this: my father and his organization of rich, influential peers had a hand in both her death and the cover up. My mother's dying words had led me on a merry fucking goose chase for a year, but I was finally making headway.

Which led me to the third instrumental moment: joining The Elite.

The wet ground sucked at my feet as I trudged through the old cemetery to the abandoned convent on the crest of a small hill. Pride was already there, his feet braced apart and tattooed arms crossed over his bulky chest. He looked like an arrogant motherfucker with his chin tilted up brutishly and eyes narrowed, but I knew it was because he felt the weight of the chip on his shoulder like Atlas carrying the heft of the world.

Mason Blackwell had always had something to prove,

and it was about time I gave him the opportunity to do just that.

"You're late, asshole," he said, but there was humor in his rough-edged southern accent.

At that point, months after our initiation, after nearly burying Rhett's dad alive, dealing with Lillian's endless manipulations, and scouring the entire fucking earth for Samuel's sister, Sabella, he knew me well enough to know I was always late.

"Then stop posing for GQ and give me my fucking task," I said, stopping beside him and propping my shoulders up against the rain-soaked wall.

The place gave me the creeps, but then, most things associated with The Elite gave me the fucking chills. I'd installed the nearly invisible cameras at the entrance to the old nunnery months ago, when Mason had tasked God with crashing Rhett's mother's car, but I hadn't had time to review the footage yet.

I was hoping for something juicy, because at this point in my quest for justice, I had fuck all to incriminate the group outside of heresy.

"Let's go inside," Mason ordered, already turning on his heel to push open the molding wooden door.

"Let's not," I suggested, cupping my hand over my lighter to burn the end of my fat joint. When I succeeded, I took a long drag of the sweet smoke and tilted my head back against the wall, turning it slowly to peer at my brother. "I think we're past the smoke and mirrors of secret society bullshit, don't you?"

Mason gritted his teeth, annoyed at my rebellion despite knowing what I was saying was true.

Finally, after months of waiting for my six brothers to

see the light, every single one of them wanted The Elite ended almost as much as I did.

If anyone had more reason than me to want their demise, it was Mason.

I knew every single detail of his forced imprisonment, from the months of isolation to the lengths he went to in his quest for information about his sister, Evelyn.

Of course, he didn't know how much I knew, and he probably wouldn't thank me for it if he did. Prideful motherfucker.

"Fine," he muttered, retrieving the old-school scroll from his pocket and handing it to me. "Let me guess, you're going to use your coin to get out of this one?"

The Elite had one 'get out of jail free' card, a silver coin imprinted with their logo that an initiate could trade in instead of completing their task.

I shrugged a shoulder as I unraveled the parchment, my joint tucked at the side of my mouth. "Depends on the task."

He scowled. "After everything that's happened with Lillian and Four, you actually want to do what The Elite is telling us to do? I've got to say, man, you're confusing as fuck. From the beginning, I couldn't get a read on you, and after talking to the others, they're just as lost. Why did you join up?"

What an easy question to answer—a question I'd read in the eyes of my brothers for weeks as I helped them through their tasks and myriads of problems.

The *why* was simple.

It was the who, how, and *when* that proved the puzzle.

Without answering him, I looked down at the open scroll and read my task.

Sloth.

Idle hands do the devil's best work.

Your task is to desecrate St. Augustine's Church.

An excess of faith in the wrong thing is sinful.

We aim to teach Archbishop Savoie the perils of being too willful.

Take his pious daughter and ruin her.

I looked up at Pride, laughter in my eyes and a smile on my lips. "You're fucking kidding me with this?"

He scowled at me, annoyed by my constant good cheer. He was a broody motherfucker. "Has anything about this seemed funny to you?"

I shrugged. because I figured he wouldn't like my honest answer. "My father has his nose so far up Archbishop Savoie's ass in his quest for an endorsement for his second term in Senate, I'm surprised the fucker can even see past his shit. He's even more zealous than normal about this campaign. He'll do anything to ensure Malcom doesn't beat him out of the Senate." I paused, looking down at the scroll again. "My father and the archbishop are part of The Elite, why would they give me a task that ruins them?"

Not that I gave a single fuck if my father was ruined, but still, something wasn't adding up, and I didn't like unsolved mysteries. It was one of the reasons I'd been sticking my nose in my other Elite brothers' business throughout the entire year.

A man with knowledge was a man with power.

Mason frowned and crossed his arms. "I think we've established I'm just the unlucky fucking messenger in this situation. The only thing I know is up until a week ago, I had a *different* envelope for you Lillian gave me, and when I went to look for it, this one was in its place in my bag."

"How do you know they're different?"

Mason's face twisted in disgust. "Lillian used to leave a red kiss mark beside the fucking seal."

I echoed his face. "What the fuck? Who would have the authority or know-how to give me a new task?"

We stared at each other for a moment. There were only two men powerful enough to stand up to Lillian: her brother and God's dad.

"Malcom or Four."

I stared at the parchment, warring with myself.

On the one hand, I wanted to fucking destroy the society, not take up their gauntlet and ruin more lives like my brothers had in their name. I could easily cash in my coin and be done with the whole fucking thing.

But…

I'd been playing the good son with my vile fucking father since the day my mother had been murdered. I'd applied to his alma mater, St. Augustine, and been accepted into his precious Elite. I'd been part of the society's disgusting actions so even if I didn't desecrate the church and defile the archbishop's daughter, it wasn't like my hands were clean.

I had my fingers in so many of The Elite's shitholes, it was a wonder I didn't stink from all their evil deeds.

This could be an opportunity to take down the real power behind The Elite, not just the witch Lillian. She was the queen of all bitches, but she didn't have the kind of power someone like Four and the upper echelons of the society must have had to wield so much control over the city.

"This is your chance to cash in the coin, dude," Mason reminded me as he watched my indecision. "Take it from someone who's done way too many fucked up things for this society, you don't want to have a ruined life on your conscience."

"God would say the say same thing," I muttered, thinking of the brother I'd most recently bonded with the most. He'd hit a girl with a fucking car a few weeks ago, cracking her open like a nut on the hood of the stolen BMW. I'd seen him after the fact, more broken spiritually than the brain-dead girl had been physically, sitting in the hospital like a condemned man. I'd also seen him yesterday when he'd stalked the girl, Zemira, through the halls of St. Augustine like a love-sick fool. "But if he never completed his task, he wouldn't have met Z."

Mason scowled at me. "That's a fucking specific example."

I torched the end of my blunt, pulling a huge drag into my lungs before blowing it out slowly into a series of perfect circles that dissolved in his face. "Rhett, Sam, and you would say the same fucking thing about you and your women."

"Fuck you." Mason grinned meanly and amended his statement. "But would Envy?"

I gritted my teeth at the mention of our lost brother. The Elite had dragged him off somewhere undisclosed, but we were bound and fucking determined to find him.

Not just because he was our seventh, but because some of us were growing more and more convinced it had been Sebastian who'd killed Sam's twin sister, Sabella.

"Five outta six isn't a bad ratio," I said, assuming my lighthearted façade again as easily as breathing.

Mason shook his head at me in disbelief. "You're so fucking chill about everything, man, sometimes I wonder if you give a shit about a fucking thing."

The feel of my mother's diamond ring on the chain around my neck burned into my skin at his words. I'd been the one to take my mother's effects from the coroner after they'd found her waterlogged body and examined it. I wore her wedding ring around my neck as a daily reminder that my father and his fucking Elite were the reason she was dead.

"I like you, man," I told Mason as I rolled up the scroll and tucked it in the back pocket of my jeans. "But you're not my fucking girlfriend, so don't expect me to tell you my heart's desires, yeah?"

Mason watched me as I backed away from him toward the parking lot where my driver was waiting with the Rolls. It was a Sunday morning, the perfect time to check out St. Augustine's Cathedral.

"The way we survive this thing is to band together, Rush. Alone, we're weak against those motherfuckers. Together, we can survive."

"I'm not in this to survive, brother. I'm in this to fucking *end* them."

VII

UINCENDUM NATUS

THREE

Rush

She was holding rosary beads the way I imagined her holding my cock, firm grip, fingers reverent and deliberate. I watched her thumb rub over and over the biggest bead closest to the delicate gold cross at its end, and I knew I had to have her.

Not because she was sexy; because she wasn't.

She was wearing a blouse tied at the neck with a thin black ribbon, like some kind of pious present offered at the altar of her God, and a long plaid skirt reminiscent of prepubescent Catholic school girls before they've been properly corrupted.

I wanted to do that—the corrupting. That's why she was sexy to me even in her prim little outfit, even with her little red mouth parted softly as she muttered fervent prayers along with Archbishop Savoie.

SLOTH

I could smell her innocence from across the massive antechamber of St. Augustine's Cathedral. Like baby's breath, both newborn and elderly in a way forbidden enough to get my dick hard.

A sharp gasp drew my attention to my right where an elderly woman across the aisle was staring at me, her beady eyes full of judgment.

I followed her gaze to the large erection straining my slacks, then looked back up at her with a wink.

"It's pierced," I mouthed.

It was a lie—no way was I sticking a needle through my dick head—but she didn't need to know that.

Her face flashed red, then white, like ambulance lights, and I wondered idly if she might be having a heart attack.

My suspicions were confirmed not thirty seconds later when she gripped her arm and fell gasping to the floor.

I watched from my slouched position in the pew as mayhem ensued, the good Catholic flock hovering over the distressed woman, holding hands as they prayed for her recovered health.

She was dead before the ambulance arrived.

It didn't shock me that I'd been her harbinger of death. I was a faithless soul with blasphemous thoughts and a sacrilegious goal. I was honestly surprised I hadn't burst into flames the moment I'd crossed the threshold of St. Augustine's to scope out my virginal little victim.

Better her than me.

I strolled out after the crush of people pushed through the wide oak doors into the humid air of an early New Orleans spring, leaning against the warm brick as I surveyed the crowd. My eyes caught on a soft cloud of golden-brown hair pulled back with a velvet ribbon. I wanted to loosen it, watch all those curls fall over her pale, naked shoulders before I retied it around her neck, a little too tightly so she'd feel me with every breath she took.

I pulled at my lower lip as I stared at the back of her head, willing her to turn around so I could see the exact shape of her mouth to imagine it wrapped around my cock later.

Coaxed by my unspoken will, she turned with a sudden breeze that ruffled her curls. She was speaking to someone, her heart-shaped face soft with sympathy as she offered some candy-coated platitudes.

Her mouth was a pale pink like the inside of a seashell, but I knew if I could get my teeth and lips on her, it would bloom red like a bleeding rose under my ministrations.

The zeal of my attraction surprised me.

I wasn't the kind of man to feel anything deeply at all.

But ever since my mother was murdered, I'd felt these odd stirrings in my gut as if something like empathy had germinated and was taking root.

I wanted to take sheers to the growth, strip it methodically of leaves, and rip out every inch of its roots so I was fallow once more.

But the girl with the ribbon seemed to trigger something inside me that felt like a flood of sunlight. Those roots deepened, the leaves unfurled.

My desire for her felt good, but deeply, elementally wrong.

As if sensing my conflict, she paused mid-speech and looked slowly over her shoulder, directly into my eyes.

Hers were large and dark in a face of porcelain.

She looked fragile; a China doll.

Something a callous man could break easily in his rough, strong hands.

I licked my lips, thinking about doing just that.

There was no doubt in my mind such a pious girl was virginal.

I'd never had one before—too much work—but the thought of smearing her wetness over my cock and defiling her with my cum was too fucking hot to bear.

I had to have her.

Not for any reason, but my own confounding yearning to take her .

Her eyes widened, and a flush settled like dusk into her white cheeks.

"Come here," I mouthed as I pulled the joint from behind my ear and rolled it between my fingers.

She hesitated, her eyes darting to the side to the older couple she had been conversing with, but they didn't notice her indecision.

When she looked back at me with wide, harried eyes, I lifted one brow in a silent dare to obey me.

She did.

The breeze swirled her long skirt around her thin legs, prompting me to imagine the kind of underwear she might be wearing beneath it.

No doubt plain white cotton or something with little flowers on it.

My dick leapt in my pants at the thought of plucking those flowers and the red bloom between her thighs.

"Can I help you with something?" she asked as she came to a stop a few cautious feet away.

Her voice was light, lilting with a faint hint of an

accent and soft with something like a lisp. It wasn't the slow syrup drip of a southern drawl or the soft twang of Cajun.

"Do you promise to help me no matter my needs?" I asked, just to watch her blush. "A good little lamb helps whenever they can, right?"

"I...well, I'd prefer to know what it is you need before I offer my services," she admitted primly. "For example, if you require something of a licentious nature, there are a number of places on Bourbon Street I could recommend."

"What does a church mouse like you know about Bourbon Street?"

She tilted her chin in haughty rebellion even as she wrung her hands nervously. They were small, with pale, dexterous fingers. I wondered if they would feel hot or cold wrapped around my dick.

"What does a sinner like you know about faith, yet here you are at St. Augustine's Cathedral?" she countered. "Believing in God doesn't mean I'm stupid or uninformed."

Doesn't it?

I didn't question her further. I could see she was gearing up for a fight, and I didn't have the energy or time for verbal warfare.

I was half an hour late for my summons at my father's office to discuss the latest way I'd disappointed him. An old friend of his was my philosophy professor and he had tattled like a child about my lack of attendance in his class.

It was easy to disguise my innate patience as laziness, and I was all too happy to do it if it meant I would be underestimated in the end. I didn't need anyone else to validate my intelligence. I had an above average score on multiple IQ tests and a successful side business in coding that spoke for themselves.

"I like to have context for my sins, otherwise how do I know I'm sinning?" I said with a lazy curl of my lips before pushing off the wall and walking toward her.

She took a stuttering step back on her Mary Jane's, but I caught her wrist before she could fall. Her skin was supple silk. I knew my fingermarks would adorn her wrist like a bracelet for the next two days.

The possessive thought sent a fucking thrill through me.

"Do you know what it is to sin, church mouse?" I caught a piece of her hair between my fingers and twirled it over my thumb. "I'm more than happy to tutor you."

She glared up at me through her long, tangled eyelashes. "I have a name. It's Isabelle Savoie. And I would offer the same service to you so you might learn the true meaning of faith, but I'm not stupid enough to believe I could ever make a difference."

I watched her move away from me with a one-shoulder shrug. "You never know, I feel pretty close to God after I make a woman come for me."

Isabelle shivered, a look of disgust marring her classically pretty face. But there was a high flush streaked like peach paint over her cheeks, and her hard nipples punched through the filmy fabric of her blouse.

She hated me on principle, but her body reacted to mine on instinct.

"You may think you fly under the radar at St. Augustine's, but I see you, Rush Dempsey. I was friends with Zemira Coleman. I saw what your friend God did to her. Don't bother telling me you're any different. I know just what kind of fornicator you are."

I threw my head back and laughed, the unfamiliar surge of humor in my throat strange and slightly painful. Tears pooled in the corners of my eyes. I braced a hand over my abs as they contracted at the force of my laughter.

When I recovered enough to look at her, she was frowning, her arms crossed like an offended old lady.

It made me chuckle again.

"*Fornicator.* Fuck me, haven't laughed like that in... maybe ever," I admitted, then narrowed my eyes as I studied the pinched set to her mouth and the way she wrung her hands together. "Have you?"

She was startled by my question. "Laughed?"

I nodded, stuffing my hands in my pockets as I slowly walked away from her. My phone buzzed in my pocket, telling me my driver was in the lot waiting for me. "Having fun isn't a sin, you know. Call me if you're ever looking for a good time."

"Like I would," she said with an eyeroll, but then her eyes darted over the dispersing crowd, and she called out, "I don't even have your number."

I grinned at her and tilted my chin. Hacking and coding were my two secret weapons. And people say spending too much time on the computer is bad for you...

"In your contacts, under the name SLOTH," I told her with a wink before I turned on the heel of my Ferragamo loafer and strolled the rest of the way to my waiting Rolls Royce.

I never expected the little church mouse to take me up on the offer, even in the weeks following when her sweet, tantalizing face brought some quality of light to my darkening existence.

I should have known better than to judge her. After all, I'd based my entire identity on a persona of indolent ennui when I was anything but lazy.

Still, the text surprised me when it came through weeks later.

Church Mouse: You said to text you for a good time. Well, *laissez les bons temps rouler*.

VII

UINCENDUM NATUS

FOUR

Isabelle

I was used to being invisible to my peers.

In fact, I preferred it that way.

Adults esteemed me for my work ethic, altruism, and good manners, but even their compliments were tepid, their regard infrequent. I was a structural pillar of my community, but not an obvious one. Everyone knew the name of Isabelle Savoie, because of my many good deeds, even though they consistently forgot the name of that sweet girl who worked at the cathedral.

I'd learned from an early age the spotlight was a dangerous place to be, and I'd adjusted accordingly. Once, I'd been an astonishingly pretty, gregarious child, and now, at the age of twenty-four, I wore the clothes of a virginal schoolgirl and the attitude of a pedantic spinster.

SLOTH

There was no reason for someone like Rush Dempsey to notice me. I walked the line of mundane so carefully, I never fell to either side of a contrast where someone might notice me.

So, why had he?

The question haunted me for days after his random foray into my father's cathedral, stalking my every thought like a sinister specter.

I couldn't wrap my head around it, and my intelligence was the only quality I allowed myself to indulge in so my lack of insight began to chafe until the question was an open sore at the back of my skull.

The only thing I knew for certain was that he was beautiful in a way that reminded me of angels. His soft swoop of golden hair pushed back from his forehead highlighted his long, thick brows and sloe-lidded eyes the color of molten chocolate. He was almost *too* pretty with his symmetrical features and pouty lower lip, but there was a sinful slant to his gaze and the steep cut of his jawbone that lent him just enough masculinity to be sheer male perfection.

I'd never noticed men before…at least, not the way I noticed Rush. His eyes on me felt too hot, the weight of them bruising against my tender skin.

A small, dark place in my gut told me I wanted that heat and those bruises.

"Isabelle," my father's voice boomed throughout the empty cathedral, ricocheting off the vaulted ceilings and echoing in the domed fresco at its apex.

I winced as I got off my knees between a row of pews where I'd been waxing the mahogany wood to a high gleam. When I turned to face him, he was already halfway across the space from his office, his thick thighs carrying him to me on brutishly large steps.

Elijah Savoie may have been the archbishop of New Orleans, the highest cleric in the state, but once, a very long time ago, he had been a running back for the football team at St. Augustine, and he still looked like it.

He had a thick neck that led to a square head on top of massive shoulders that looked frankly bizarre under his elaborate red silk robes. It was his hands, though, that gave away his brute strength. They were thickly quilted with muscle in the palms and corded with veins that throbbed when he was angry enough to fist them. His fingers were long, blunt weapons, heavy and without elegance.

I knew to keep an eye on those hands.

They were loose by his sides as he powered over to me, so I relaxed slightly.

"Why is it taking you so long to do your normal chores today?" he asked, frowning. "Have you been daydreaming?"

"No, they were just dirtier than usual," I explained.

It was a lie.

I never lied to my father. Heck, I never lied to anyone.

Already, just the thought of Rush Dempsey was corrupting me.

"It doesn't matter. I'll get one of the girls to do it tomorrow. Come with me now. There's someone I want you to meet," he ordered.

"Who?" I made the mistake of questioning.

He glowered at me. "You know the important work I do for the church. You also know I can't speak about much that I do. And more, you know not to question your father or the voice of God, of whom I am the mouthpiece."

SLOTH

"Yes, Father," I said meekly.

"Watch yourself, Isabelle. You've been acting out lately, and I won't have it. I need you to be on your best behavior for this visitor. He's a very powerful man in the organization I'm part of and we need his favor," he commanded, clamping one of his strong hands over my wrist and tugging me toward the left side of the chamber where his office lay.

I followed after him, casting a look over my shoulder to make sure we were alone.

We weren't.

A young man with a tragic expression on his handsome face stared unblinking at the Virgin Mary on the altar. Sensing my gaze, his eyes flickered over to me, and he frowned at my dad's hand on my arm before I was dragged behind a column, disappearing down the hall.

He wouldn't come after me to check if I was being manhandled.

No one ever did.

My dad was the archbishop of the most powerful city in the state and his flock was loyal to him to the point of cultish furor.

He knew how to command a room with his piety just as easily as he commanded me with his hands.

We pushed through the door to his office, and I saw the reason for his good mood.

A handsome man with slashing black brows that made him look slightly villainous and a suit I could tell was absurdly expensive even with my lack of fashion knowledge sat in my father's chair behind the desk as if it was his office and not the archbishop's.

He smiled thinly at me as his eyes raked over my modestly dressed form.

"Isabelle, I want you to meet my good friend, Malcom Benedict," my dad said proudly, shoving me forward by the small of my back to present me. "Malcom, my daughter and St. Augustine Cathedral's administrator, Isabelle."

Malcom didn't stand. Instead, he looked over my body once more before shooting a vaguely disgusted look at my dad.

"Malcom Benedict III, Elijah, and I would certainly not call you a good friend." After dressing him down, Malcom stood and buttoned his blazer before stepping forward to take my hand in both of his.

They were so cold, they made me shudder.

"Isabelle," he said, tasting the word on his tongue, then adjusting his mouth so the next time he said it, the three syllables rolled even more elegantly off his tongue. "Isabelle Savoie, the young and beautiful church mouse of St. Augustine and diligent student at our city's most prestigious university. How do you do it?"

Warning bells rattled in my brain at his use of the same nickname Rush had given me a few weeks ago. Did they know each other?

"How can I help you, Mr. Benedict III?" I asked softly.

In my experience, a soft voice and a sweet smile would give a woman the advantage over any man, however powerful. It was as instinctual for them to treat me with condescension as it was for adults to coo over puppies and newborns. And it was exactly that condescension that made them vulnerable to me, because it meant they didn't think I was a smart enough or important enough to be careful around.

"I'm a...problem solver of sorts. I always have been. Only now, I'm going into office. I expect there to be a radical shift in the state government within the next few weeks, and I want to be ready to take up the torch when I'm called to do so."

"What is it exactly you need from me?" I asked, my gumption as newborn and fragile as a budded rose.

Malcom's mirthless smile sliced across his face like a wound he wanted to inflict on others. "I wanted to see for myself what my competitor wants to use against me."

I tried to tug my hand away from his grip, but his fingers tightened.

"You know, in a strange way, you're almost worth the effort to defile myself," he mused casually, as if his words didn't strike horror in my soul.

"See here, Malcom, you told me you wanted to offer for her yourself," my dad blustered from behind me, stepping up to wrench me away from the other man's grip.

Malcom's smile froze into place, then shattered into a vicious glare. "If you dare touch me again, Elijah, I will strip you of your position in the church and your minimal standing in The Elite as easily as I breathe. Is that understood?"

For the first time in my life, I watched my dad's florid complexion turn ashen with fear. He nodded and swallowed heavily.

"I can see your dear old dad hasn't explained this to you," Malcom continued, as if my father hadn't interrupted. "But he's made a deal with a very specific brand of devil, and you are the price he was all too willing to pay."

"Wh-What are you talking about?" I stuttered, succumbing to my childhood affliction. I felt as afraid and vulnerable as a little girl.

He reached out to clasp my limp hand again, giving it a pitying pat. "At the end of this, I've no doubt you'll be ruined either way. You've got a choice, and the only one is this: Sloth or Pride?"

I swallowed thickly as he abruptly dropped my hand and walked straight passed me out the door.

"Dad, what is he talking about?" I asked as I turned to look at him.

He had the ornate gold cross he wore around his neck clutched in one hand as if it would bring him salvation from his own utterance. "One of my flock came to me asking to take you on a date. I told him I was happy for him to do so because I know him to be a good man with fortune and favor in New Orleans. I think you'll like him."

"Why did that man come in and make such a big production of it?" I asked, because my dad had set me up with members of his congregation before.

"This man is a bit…long in the tooth."

"You mean old." I didn't think I'd mind an older man. I'd been raised to be serious and mature. In fact, an older man could suit me very well. "How old?"

My dad hesitated, then straightened his chin and fisted his hands into hammers. "Old enough to have a son younger than you."

I gaped at him. "And who is it?"

"Senator Dempsey," he said. "Ward Dempsey."

I had never met Ward before, but I'd heard of him. Everyone in New Orleans knew Senator Dempsey. He was the most successful Senator our state had seen in years, including, but not limited to, his success passing a state bill for school funding that would increase our low graduation rates by a projected 33.3%.

That wasn't the only way I knew Ward, though.

His wife, Magnolia, had been on the head of our charitable division at the church. We'd spent many hours working side by side, both in my cramped office and at St. Augustine's Orphanage.

She'd been a lovely woman, beautiful inside and out, but tragic like something out of a Shakespeare play. She never discussed much about her personal life, only a few comments here and there about her four sons, but whenever Ward was brought up, she'd tense.

I recognized the posture because I did the same thing whenever my father clenched his fists.

I wasn't sure if he'd physically, mentally, or emotionally abused Magnolia, but he'd certainly scared her in a way she couldn't easily hide.

I stared at the handsome, wealthy man sitting across from me in one of New Orleans' most popular restaurants, and I couldn't help but be scared too.

"You're beautiful, like your mother was." He smiled charmingly as the server presented us with our drinks.

Mine was non-alcoholic because I didn't drink.

"I'm not," I admitted. "Though, I can't say I try as hard as she did."

Ward laughed, the first genuine expression in the twenty minutes we'd been together since he picked me up from my small house tucked behind the cathedral gardens.

"Yes, I remember Joie was rather vain."

"She was terrifying," I said blandly, surprised again when he laughed.

"You must miss her," he said after he sobered.

"I must," I agreed simply.

There was something about him that seemed dishonest, a static quality to his smile, as if he wore it often and by rote instead of being honestly amused or pleased with something.

It definitely didn't compare to his son's pouty grin.

I winced internally at the thought.

There I was on a date with his father and I was thinking about him.

"You have a son?" I asked innocently, unable to help myself.

Ward's smile widened. "Four, actually. They're shaping up to be amazing men, at least the first of them."

"Not the last?"

His smile dulled and he focused on taking a sip of his manly cocktail before answering. "Rush was spoiled by his mother as a boy. He doesn't understand the value of hard work." He looked up into my eyes with a tilt of his chin. "Not like we do."

"'Diligent hands will rule, but laziness ends in forced labor,' Proverbs 10:4-5," I quoted from the Bible.

"And you desire to rule, do you, Isabelle?" he asked, a sudden intensity making him sit straighter and lean closer to me.

"No, not at all. I desire to rule my own destiny, to carve out the type of person I strive to be and the kind of life I want to lead by my own hard work and volition."

"Well there's nothing so hard about that," Ward said, leaning back again, clearly disappointed.

"Excuse me for saying so, but only someone who has been born into wealth and power would say that."

Ward's brows lifted slightly, but his forehead didn't crease and I realized with slight revulsion that he'd had Botox or something done.

"Your circumstances are what you make of them."

"And sometimes the circumstances are so dire, it takes a little longer to make something out of them," I retorted gently.

Ward blinked at me, seemingly deciding whether he would admire my logic or castigate me for it.

Finally, a small smile broke across his lips. "Well, I should expect as much for a theologian."

"What should I expect from a politician?" I asked, my confidence growing. There was something about the man that made me restless and irritated, ready for a fight. I was no pugilist, but I could hold my own with words. "You asked my father to take me out today for some reason. I doubt it's because of my beauty, so what is it exactly you want from me?"

His fingers stroked the side of his rocks glass, and I noticed there was still a slight tan on his left ring finger from his wedding ring. He'd only been a widow for one year and he was back on the hunt.

I was no Magnolia Dempsey. I didn't have her elegance, her sophisticated hauteur, or her good looks.

So, what then?

"I know this probably seems slightly archaic to you, but alliances such as these have been making the world go round for centuries. Even now, in the modern age, in the highest reaches of society, we make decisions based on more than just love and beauty. We make matches because of the connections they will bring us."

"Ah," I said, understanding. "You want my father to endorse your senate re-election."

Ward inclined his head in agreement. "I do. You're also as pure as the driven snow and a familiar beacon of goodness in New Orleans. You'll do well as a political wife."

"And if I wasn't so pure?" I asked recklessly, my heart-rate jumping from a canter straight through to a gallop that reverberated through my ribcage.

I didn't want to be a political pawn in the games my father played.

I didn't want to go from one power hungry man to another.

This time, when Ward smiled, it wasn't magazine ready perfection. It was as sharp as a weapon aimed right at my jugular.

"You're old enough to know about the society your father is a part of, aren't you, Isabelle?" When I nodded hesitantly, he continued. "Well, let's just say I'm a powerful member of that society and your father owes me some significant favors for elevating him into his position and keeping all his dirty secrets swept tidily under the rug. Your father was Envy, and I was Pride, in a position to do things for him. If you do anything stupid to break this alliance, I'll have to break him."

I could have told him I didn't care if he broke my father, that far from caring about his wellbeing, the darkest, most sinful pieces of my heart actually yearned for his re-crimination after the years of abuse I'd taken at his hands.

But I didn't.

Ward had exposed his vulnerabilities to me because

he thought I was lesser—a weak woman with no spine or brain to carry her independently through life without a man to control her.

He didn't know I was smart and capable, that my lack of fashion and the softness of my expressions didn't mean I was meek.

It meant I was a lion dressed as a lamb.

Ward excused himself to go to the restroom, and I watched him walk off as a bead of sweat dripped down my temple.

There was really only one plan available to me, and it meant the end of my life as I knew it.

I could choose Ward and his Pride, as Malcom Benedict had said.

Or Rush and his Sloth.

My sweaty fingers slipped on my ancient green and white flip phone as I pulled it from my purse and typed out the sentence that would plot a different course for my destiny than I had ever imagined before.

At least I was the one doing the navigating.

Me: You said to text you for a good time. Well, *laissez les bons temps rouler.*

VII

U I N C E N D U M   N A T U S

FIVE

Rush

"Tell me you found her," I ordered the girl with pink, purple, and orange dreadlocks across from me. "Tell me you found Sabella."

"Buy me bananas foster first," she demanded, getting to her knees on the chair in the elegant dining room so she could flag down a waiter. "I heard they were invented here."

I sighed heavily. I knew Harriet wouldn't give me any information unless I fed her first. She was the best hacker and private investigator I knew, but her professionalism left a lot to be desired.

"They were. New Orleans was one of the biggest trading posts for bananas when they first began importing them, and the owner of Brennan's challenged his chef to make a dish that featured them."

Harriet blinked her huge blue eyes at me.

"You knew that already," I surmised. "Of course, you did. You always make me take you to the touristy fucking places in the city."

She shrugged. "I'm from Minnesota. I'm trying to acclimate to the culture."

I rolled my eyes. "You've been here for ten years, Harry, I think you've about done it."

She flashed a cheeky grin, but stayed silent while I ordered her the bananas foster and got myself a coffee.

Only when she was happily tucked into her caramelized bananas and ice cream did she start speaking.

"Think I got her."

I perked up slightly out of my slouch. "Are you sure?"

She wiped her cream-smeared mouth with the back of her hand. "No, I said *think*. If I was sure, I'd have said 'I'm sure I got her.'"

"Jesus, Harry, just fucking lay it out for me."

"I think the church might be involved. St. Augustine's Cathedral," she said with her mouth full. "Does that make any sense to you?"

A chill slid like an ice cube down my back. I inclined my chin in agreement.

"I haven't been able to figure it out yet. All I know is someone of Sabella Gunnar's description was seen by witnesses near the residence dorms *after* she was supposed to have been killed."

"That means shit all," I growled. "Witnesses are unreliable. You are always the first to say that."

She raised a purple eyebrow at me. "I've never seen you this animated about something before. What's this girl to you?"

"Nothing," I retorted automatically.

But that wasn't true. Not really. At least…not anymore.

My brothers meant something to me. They were flawed fucking assholes most of the time, but compared to the shit family I'd been born into, I'd take them any day.

And Sabella meant something, almost *everything*, to Sam.

I had to get her back.

"She's basically family," I muttered, uncharacteristically embarrassed because I knew how my long-time acquaintance would react.

She proved me right by laughing her fucking face off.

"She your girlfriend or something, Rush?" she asked through her guffaws. People in the expensive dining room turned to glare at her with reproach, but she didn't care.

"No. She was Envy's," I reminded her coolly. "And look how that turned out."

She stopped laughing immediately. "Ah…well, *him*, I did find."

I froze. "Are you fucking kidding me?"

Happily, she shook her head. "No, man, I found Envy in a fucking mental hospital out of state." She dipped her hand into the pocket of her loose jeans and came up with a folded piece of paper that she slid across the table to me. "The address."

Fuck.

She actually found him.

I considered my options. I could text the guys, round them up, and we could leave like Robin Hood's merry band of idiots on a road trip to find Envy together, but there was no doubt in my mind Sam, in all his considerable wrath, would fucking end Sebastian then and there without asking any questions.

And we needed answers.

God's dad had reined in some control over Lillian, but there were still forces at play beyond our control and they all had to pay for what they'd done to us and ours.

Most of all, we needed to know what had happened to Sabella and who had been involved.

I surprised myself with my selfless line of thinking. Up until recently, my biggest and only concern was for unraveling the mystery of my mother's death.

It seemed I'd made like the Grinch and my heart had expanded to include the five bastards—excluding Envy—who had become my new family.

"I'll go alone," I decided out loud.

Harriet shrugged as she swiped her finger in the leftover melted ice cream clinging to the bowl. "I would. Your friend Samuel has a serious temper and there isn't much doubt in my mind Envy killed or seriously maimed his sister, Sabella."

"What aren't you telling me?"

"I broke into his house. Someone did a pretty thorough job of cleaning up the place with bleach, but I still caught traces of blood. A lot of it."

I closed my eyes, wishing to hell I wasn't sober enough for that to puncture my armor of numbness. If Sabella was dead, a part of Sam would die too.

"I'll leave tomorrow," I told her. "Meanwhile, I want you to find George Griffin. His daughter Chasity told us he fled the state, but I want to know the motherfucker's whereabouts. Also, you've been quiet on Lillian Griffin. There's a reason she is the way she is, and I want to know why."

"Yes, Commander Dempsey," Harriet said with a mock salute, teasing me doubly by doing that because it was a habitual gesture of mine. "I will get right on it. Next time, you can take me for hickory coffee and beignets at Café du Monde."

"We've been there six times already," I bitched.

She shrugged. "Those powdered fried delights are addictive, what can I say?"

I had no response. I hadn't been addicted to anything in my entire life. Nothing kept my interest long enough to become a passion, and I'd never enjoyed anything, maybe save weed, enough to make it an addiction.

As if the God I didn't believe in heard my thoughts and decided to test my resolve, my phone buzzed with an incoming text.

I read the popular New Orleans' expression three times before comprehending Isabelle Savoie, the same little church mouse who'd condemned me for my sins weeks ago at St. Augustine's Cathedral, was asking me to show her how to have a good time.

Me: Where are you?

I waited, pulling at my lower lip as I watched the screen for her response.

My cock was already half hard in my jeans.

Her idea of a good time was probably knitting a fucking scarf for the poor or reading to the blind, but my devious nature conjured up images of a more conjugal nature.

I wanted her prone, prostrate against the alter, her milky thighs parted like the pages of a bible for me to defile with my tongue.

Church Mouse: I'm actually on a date with your father at Brennan's.

SLOTH

Immediately, my head shot up from my phone, swiveling around the huge, crowded restaurant until I spotted her tucked into the far corner dressed in something that resembled my deceased grandmother's old curtains.

"You'll excuse me, Harry," I told her without bothering to look at her. I threw down enough cash to cover the meal with a huge tip, then stalked through the dining room to Isabelle's side.

She only noticed me when I was a foot away from the table, her small, perfectly bowed mouth parting on a gasp.

I wanted to slide my fingers, tongue, and cock into that mouth and test their fit.

"Rush?" she asked in her sweet, French accented voice.

I nodded, then held out my hand to her, silently asking her to leave with me.

There was fury in my heart at the idea of my father spending any amount of time with this woman. I wanted to get us safely out of their before he returned from whatever phone call had taken him away from her.

He should have known better than to leave his prey alone. Another predator might just swoop in and snatch her up.

Isabelle stared at my hand as if it was an alien thing, something threatening and unknown.

"You can take it," I told her quietly, soothingly. "I won't hurt you."

She bit her lip as she looked between my eyes and my hand before finally slipping her cold, smooth hand over my palm.

I angled our hands until I could intertwine our fingers, then gave her a squeeze.

"Good?" I asked, surprised by my own chivalry. When she nodded, I started to pull her behind me out of the restaurant. *"Alors, lassiez les bons temps rouler!"*

I was usually slow, methodical in my approach to a problem. I surveyed all the angles, digested all the options, until the proper solution rouse seamlessly to the surface.

I did not do that with Isabella Savoie.

There was something about her gentleness and reserve that surged through me like an excess of endorphins. I felt both high on her unassuming loveliness and more sober than I'd ever been before because I was constantly aware of protecting her from the world around her.

If anyone was going to show her a good time, it would be me, and absolutely no one else.

We went bar hopping.

She'd never had an alcoholic beverage before, and the woman was older than me. When she hesitated in accepting the hurricane I bought for us to share at Pat O'Brien's, I placed my hand over both of her small ones and cradled them.

"I know I'm the worst kind of fornicator," I told her in a low rumble beneath the cacophony of late afternoon traffic in the busy bar, "but I won't take advantage of you—not unless you ask me to."

A tremulous smile spread across her face, dissolving any idea in my mind that Isabelle was anything other than gorgeous. "You're charming when you put your mind to it."

"I don't usually turn my mind to anything, so you must be the exception," I told her as I handed her the hurricane lamp shaped glass filled with vibrant red liquid. "It's a typical New Orleans drink, any tourist will tell you." She giggled when I winked at her. "It's sweet, though, so it's a good drink to lose your virginity to."

She paused in taking a long pull from the swirly straw, her cheeks flushing the same color as the drink. "Would you be just as sweet?"

I almost choked on my tongue at her dirty innuendo said in the lilting voice of an angel. Half the blood from my brain rushed to my cock, and I shifted my hips toward the bar so she wouldn't see my half-chub and freak out.

"I don't think anyone has accused me of such a thing before," I offered honestly. "But for you, I could try."

"This is good," she said a few minutes later after sucking back half the drink. "Really yummy."

I bit the edge of my smile so she wouldn't think I was making fun of her, but she was just too fucking cute.

"So, you going to tell me why the fuck you were on a date with my father?" I asked, keeping my voice light so she wouldn't suspect the inferno of rage building in my belly.

My father was clearly drawn to pure women with good hearts. My mother had exhibited some of the same qualities as Isabelle. Both were kind, gentle, soft spoken, but smart.

Obviously, he took some sick delight in ruining the lives of women like that.

A fierce surge of protectiveness branded itself into my bones.

There was no way in heaven or hell I was going to let anyone fuck with this girl.

Not my father.

Not The Elite.

Not even myself.

If I was going to pursue the strangely provocative church mouse, I was going to do it as a good man, the kind of man I'd witness all my brothers becoming as they met and wooed their women over the last few months.

First, I had to figure out what my dad wanted with her, who had given me the task to destroy her and her father, and *why*.

"I think he wants to marry me," she admitted sheepishly before using her lips to capture the straw and suck it back into her mouth.

I tried not to be distracted by her unconsciously sexy gesture, focusing on the absurdity of her words. "Are you fucked?"

She scowled at me. "I am definitely not. Virginal as they come. That's why he wants me, you know, because I am 'as pure as the driven snow' or something." She frowned in adorable confusion and I realized she was already drunk off half the drink.

Gently, I unpeeled her fingers from the glass and took it away from her.

"That's why I texted you," she continued, leaning over the sticky bar and looking left and right for a bartender. When she saw one, she waved excitedly for him to come closer. While we waited, she explained, "I knew you could corrupt a girl in your sleep with eyes like that."

I raised an eyebrow in question when she shot a quick glance my way.

"Your eyes," she explained, as if it was obvious. "I think people call them 'bedroom eyes.'"

I chuckled as the bartender finally approached her.

"Excuse me, may I please have another of those drinks," she asked, pointing to the hurricane in my hand. "He stole mine."

This time, my laugh escaped me like a herd of elephants trampling over my tongue. I clutched at my gut as it contracted painfully, unused to the feeling.

Fuck me, but I hadn't laughed that hard in years.

Isabelle was frowning at me like a prim school marm when I recovered enough to look over at her. There was a new drink in her hand, and she already had the straw tucked between her pink lips.

"I was being serious—about the bedroom eyes thing," she reprimanded me softly. "I knew if anyone could tarnish my reputation, it would be you."

"Here I was thinking my sex tape made the best resume, but it's my bedroom eyes, huh?" I could practically *feel* my eyes twinkling at her like some kind of besotted fool.

I felt like one.

That burgeoning sapling of emotiveness in my chest unfurled farther, extending tenuous green branches into my chest, budding against my heart.

There was something about the girl that transcended my cynicism and studied boredom, that spoke to a part of me I couldn't keep shielded from feeling.

"You have a sex tape?" she gasped as her eyes turned huge like twin chocolate coins.

A laugh rumbled through me. "I didn't set out to make it, but yeah, I do. Pretty sure you couldn't find it online anymore if you tried, though. My dad got it taken down."

"A sex tape," she murmured, studying me with wide

eyes, as if I was a new person standing beside her. "Wow. I definitely chose the right person to corrupt me."

"Jesus," I moaned, thinking of all the ways I would do just that.

"You shouldn't take the Lord's name in vain," she scolded, then bit her lip. "I sound like a seventy-year-old woman, don't I?"

"A little bit," I agreed, but I hated the way her face crumpled with self-reproach. Reaching out, I fingered one of the curls that fell around her face from beneath her velvet headband. "It definitely makes the age difference sexier."

Even her chuckle seemed accented and chic, spilling from between her lips like champagne bubbles.

"I can't be that much older than you," she protested. "Your father is a lot older than me."

"And he's never getting his hands on you," I promised somberly before lightening the mood by stepping back and stroking my chin like an ancient philosopher. "How old do you think I am?"

"You're too goofy to be older than twenty-one."

I nodded with faux gravitas. "Sure, sure, but you haven't seen me undressed yet. I think you'd have a different opinion of me then."

Her throat tightened as she swallowed thickly. Her eyes danced dangerously close to my dick. "Um, maybe, but for now, I'm going to say you're twenty."

"Nineteen," I corrected.

"So, you act like a kid, and I act like a retiree," she mused, her tongue sticking out to grasp the straw on her already half-finished drink. "Maybe we should meet in the middle."

SLOTH

I stepped into her space, a hand curling around her hip to draw her up against the erection pressing through my jeans. She gasped softly, but I angled my head down until my lips were a breath away from hers. "I'd love to meet you in the middle."

She stared up at me as I pulled away, her eyes pale brown and glowing like maple syrup caught in sunlight.

"I don't know what I've gotten myself into," she confessed. "I feel like I'm having an out-of-body experience."

"Me too," I admitted. "Are you afraid?"

She nodded. "My life is boring, but there's safety in predictability."

"My life is insane, but I've never really cared," I told her, feeling the closed book I'd always kept locked in my chest creak open, the spine cracking for the first time. "Then my mom died last year and things started to change."

Isabelle's hand slid over my cheek into my hair so she could bring me closer to her serious gaze. I read what she wrote for me there, her empathy and apology, her sorrow and platonic love for a fellow human in distress. There was so much goodness in her heart, it shone through her eyes and bathed me like noon sunshine.

I shuddered and blinked away the sunspots in my vision, stepping back to get some much-needed distance. My body was edgy with unused energy, my mind pinging like an out-of-control squash ball in an empty court.

I needed an outlet, and I couldn't get high, not around the church mouse, so instead, I turned to the discarded, melted hurricane on the table and sucked it back in three swallows. Wiping the back of my forearms over my mouth, I tossed money on the bar and grabbed Isabelle's hand.

"Enough talking, let's get you a little dirty."

VII

UINCENDUM NATUS

SIX

Isabelle

S inning with a practiced sinner was easier than it should have been.

We went carousing up and down Bourbon Street with the rest of the early spring tourists, drinking sugary drinks out of enormous funnel-like plastic glasses while listening to the street bands and indulging in endless cocktails at some of the city's craziest bars. By the time the sun had set, I was drunk as a skunk and happier than I'd ever been in my entire life.

It confused and upset me that my happiness possibly derived from libation. It felt hollow and unhealthy to say getting drunk meant getting happy.

Rush laughed with a man across the room, the one who had been playing one of the pianos on the main stage when we first entered. He looked carefree and flushed with pleasure, his golden hair in disarray and white dress shirt rolled up over his tanned forearms. My heart tripped and stuttered, then restarted again at the sight of him like that, happy with me, with our night of debauchery.

Maybe it was the alcohol making me feel newborn and delightfully alive.

Maybe it was the man leading me down the path, smiling at me through the darkness like Satan leading me into the bowls of hell.

Only, the devil wasn't horns and talons, brimstone and ash.

He was golden and gorgeous, sinning and sex.

And I was his latest victim.

I watched without breathing as he turned away from the man and made his way back to our little table with two drinks in his hands.

"I shouldn't," I said immediately. "I'm awfully drunk already."

His smile was a whisper on his lips as he held up the glass for my perusal. "Water," he said, before sliding it in front of me. "I don't want you to get sick on your first night of fun."

"Thank you," I muttered, suddenly too shy to look at him.

I was hyper aware of what he was doing, tuning my body like an instrument so I would produce a deeper, darker note when played, less heavenly minstrels and more rocking bass. Those thoughts led me to wonder what his hands would feel like playing over my skin, plucking at my nipples and strumming between my legs...

"My church mouse is blushing like she's thinking very sinful thoughts," Rush's voice interrupted my day-dreaming, dousing me in the cold waters of reality.

"A momentary lapse," I noted primly.

"Don't think of it as a lapse. How are you going to be corrupted if you don't embrace the change of lifestyle? Drinking with a friend or thinking about sex isn't going to send you straight to hell."

"Coming from a man who doesn't believe in it," I muttered. "I've spent my whole life living according to the Bible so my soul would stay pure and I'd be accepted into Heaven."

"Why?" he asked, taking a sip from his water.

I watched his plush mouth cup the rim of the glass and wondered what it might feel like cupping my lips.

"Why?" I was startled by the question. No one had ever asked me *why* I believed in God, why I was devout. Everyone I knew, minus Rush now, was a faithful Catholic.

"Yeah, why? Did you discover God after a trauma? Are you drawn to the simple nature of His rules, right vs. wrong, according to whoever wrote the Bible? *Why?*"

I felt defensive without understanding why. Did I need a reason to believe in God? He certainly didn't seem to need a reason *not* to.

The more I thought about it, though, the more the new path forged by my drunken mind took me to a disquieting realization.

I believed in God because I had faith that all living beings were connected by a higher power, that there was some cosmic force that worked toward the good of us all.

But I was an extreme devout because I had never

been given a choice otherwise. My father had dictated my relationship with religion like a football coach with his player in a game. It was his voice in my ear telling me God wouldn't love me if I didn't obey my father, my elders, and St. Augustine Cathedral's particular brand of worship.

I looked up at Rush, surprised to find my eyes damp with unshed tears. As I explained my revelation to him in a tear-soaked voice, he reached over the table and held my hand. His was strong, but graceful, with wide palms and long, tapered fingers. It felt good to have his warm skin against mine. I found myself turning my hand over so we could link fingers again.

It shouldn't have felt so life-altering to divulge the dynamics of my faith to a faithless man while twining our fingers together like links in a strong chain, but it did.

It felt like I was giving something of myself to him and he was accepting it without judgement. More than that, with reverence, because I was trusting him with me.

"It just never occurred to me to practice any other way," I finished explaining. "My father is...demanding and mercurial, so it just seemed easier to do it by the book."

"Literally," Rush said with a wry grin. "Literally do it by *his* version of the Bible."

I shrugged, exhausted by my confessions. "I guess."

"How is it that you want to be corrupted, Isabelle? I've brought you out on a night of drinking in the most anti-you part of town, but even if you go home stinking of booze, your father won't cast you out and my father won't leave you alone. If you want to get out of their clutches, you needed to make an irrevocable statement."

I sniffed. "Like a sex tape?"

He frowned down at our hands, then unclasped them. "No, not a sex tape."

I didn't listen to him. The idea had germinated in the alcoholic fertilized soil of my mind and taken root.

A sex tape with Rush Dempsey would obliterate any future my father or Ward could possibly have planned for me.

I'd be ruined, pinned with the scarlet letter for all to see.

"No," Rush repeated. "You don't understand the ramifications of what you think you want. We aren't underage. I can't just get it taken off the internet once you've made your point."

"We don't need to upload it to the internet, we just need to threaten them with it!" I cried, stoked by my own genius.

"No."

"Yes!"

"No."

"One-hundred-percent yes."

"Okay, I'm not going to play this childish game with you," Rush said, but there was amusement in his voice, and I couldn't believe I was making someone like him laugh.

That I was making anyone laugh, actually.

"Okay, y'all, I hope you're ready for a treat because we have a special guest coming up for one of our famous piano duels. Help me welcome to the stage, Rush Dempsey!" the piano player called into the microphone.

I stared in shock as Rush grinned lazily and unravelled from his slouched position in the chair.

"I expect a standing ovation," he said with a wink before he turned and strolled up the stage as if he owned it.

He clasped hands with the other pianist, then took his place at the white piano facing the other man's black one.

I didn't realize I was holding my breath until the soft strains of Eurythmics' "Sweet Dreams" drifted through the suddenly quiet bar.

Rush didn't suit his name in any way I could find until that moment. His fingers spilled over the keys like rushing water, fluid and quick. He was a natural talent, yet he didn't look as if he was exerting himself at all. There was an easy grin curling his full mouth, and his posture was still slouched. He was singing softly to the song, his voice like smoke, smooth, dark, and curling through the bar.

I could hear a few women exclaiming how beautiful he was, how he looked like an angel sitting there at that white piano playing as if he'd been born to do it.

They didn't know he was no angel.

He was a gorgeous sinner, a siren of fault and virtue who sang to something inside my heart that yearned for that duality.

He wasn't all bad, and I wasn't all good.

We could be both, maybe even together.

I listened to the lyrics of the song he'd decided to play and knew he played it for us. We were both pawns on a board, but together, we could turn the tables and find the path to the kind of life we both wanted to lead for ourselves.

While the other pianist finished with a flourish, Rush

carried out the last notes of the song by looking through the darkness of the lounge until his eyes found mine, then he sang to me alone.

Everyone was looking for something.

And Rush had just officially signed up to help me find that thing for myself.

VII

UINCENDUM NATUS

SEVEN

Rush

I watched Isabelle as she took in the luxury of my Rolls from the inside, sitting beside me in her prim headband and ridiculous granny dress. Her cheeks were flushed from the booze, her eyes bright with wonder as they skimmed the white and black leather interior, built-in televisions, and small mini bar. I was drawn to her childlike wonder at everything I had always taken for granted like a moth to a flame. There was something magic about her, just as there had been something magical about my mother.

I didn't want the magic for myself; I wanted the show of it to be performed for me and me alone.

She looked over at me and instantly blushed at the expression on my face. "You look as if you want to devour me."

I raised an eyebrow, but didn't move out of my half-sprawled position. "Maybe that's because I do."

"Smooth operator," she noted.

I shrugged. "I haven't been truly hungry for anything in my entire life."

She side-eyed me, suspicious again now that we were separated from the crowds and enclosed in darkness. It was the animal part of her brain that sensed she was under threat.

I had one arm thrown over the back of her seat, and I allowed myself to finger through the side of her curls. At first, she tensed, but when she realized I didn't mean to do anything else, she relaxed.

"You're nervous. What are you afraid I'm going to do to you?"

She licked her lips. "I think it's more what I'm afraid I'm going to do to you."

I swallowed my chuckle. "Oh?"

She faced me, a miserable expression on her face as she nodded. "I really want to kiss you right now."

I raised both my hands wide. "By all means."

"The only boy I've kissed was a choir boy when I was twelve and I called it 'slime and daggers' after that," she admitted artlessly.

Fuck me, but I loved her candor.

"It won't be like that this time," I promised her huskily. "This time will be like…silk and sunshine."

"I didn't figure you as being romantic," she breathed as she angled herself into the waiting cage of my arms.

I closed them around her tightly, one at her small waist and the other fisted in her riot of long, soft curls.

"I'm not," I said against her satin lips, teasing us both. "I'm more of a fire and brimstone man, myself."

She giggled, and the sweet sound went straight to my dick.

"It's you who'll bring the silk and sunshine." I flicked my tongue over the seam of her lips. "I'll bring the heat."

She gasped, and I took the opportunity to tighten my fist in her hair, angling her head so I could seal my mouth to hers in a conquering kiss.

My tongue slid inside her sweet mouth, and I knew immediately I'd been right.

I could live in that kiss, plundering that silken mouth, tasting her sunny essence on my tongue.

The moment our mouths met, everything else fell away.

My vendetta against The Elite, my agony over the death of my mom, my hatred for my father, my concern over Sam and the lost Sabella.

There was nothing but the gentle, absurdly erotic church mouse trapped in my embrace.

Instantly, she melted in my arms like candle wax held too close to the flame. Her hot, supple body spilled into my lap as she crawled closer, pressing so intimately to my erection, I wondered if she would be frightened off. Instead, she wrenched a groan from my throat when she adjusted to straddle my hips and lowered herself even more comfortably over my straining cock.

"That's right," I rasped as I took her hips in my hands, encouraging her to grind over my dick. "Ride me just like that."

She panted against my mouth, all inhibitions eviscerated either by the strength of the alcohol or her desire to be corrupted, to live a little before her choices were taken out of her own hands.

"One day," I told her, pausing to nip her plump lower lip between my teeth just to hear that pretty gasp of hers again. "I'll sit back just like this and make you strip for me. You'll blush and tremble, but I like that, darlin'. It shows me how excited you are. When you're naked, you'll crawl over my lap and take out my hard cock." I pressed my hips tight against her groin so she could feel the entire granite length of me. "It's big, and it'll be a struggle for your tiny pussy, but you'll be so gloriously wet and so fucking eager, you'll sit yourself down on it and work until I'm balls deep inside you."

Isabelle tucked her heated cheek against my neck as she left out a soft whimper, clearly embarrassed by my dirty talk even as she ground herself harder against my lap.

"Are you ashamed of how excited you are by the idea?" I rumbled through my tight chest.

I'd never been more turned on in my life than I was now, with this thin, pious woman dry humping me through my jeans and her distractingly patterned dress.

I hummed as I moved the collar of her dress aside to press a kiss to her shoulder while using my other hand to raise the hem of her skirt over her thigh. She buried her face deeper into my neck as I skimmed my fingers up the inside of her dewy soft thigh to the edge of her cotton underwear.

Brushing my fingers back and forth over the elastic edge and the faint downy curls there, I asked her, "Are you embarrassed that you're too wet for me? Because there is no such thing, darlin'. I want you drenched and ready for my dick to split you open for the first time."

"Oh my..." she groaned into my skin.

"God?" I asked, hiding my smug smile in her baby's breath fragrant hair. "I can be your God, darlin', but my religion is about worshipping every inch of your body and having you pray at mine."

"Don't be blasphemous," she whispered, true to her faith even in the throes of her passion.

"Do I seem like the kind of man who cares what God might think of me?" I asked her before tracing the shell of her ear with my tongue.

It shouldn't have, but it turned me on even more to have her be a good little Catholic girl while I curled my fingers around the crotch of her panties and slid to my first knuckle into her creamy heat.

"You can call out the name of your God or any other, you can sin or preach or do whatever the fuck you want while you're with me like this, Isabelle," I said, finally forcing her head back with a hand in her hair so she had to look me in the eye. Hers were dark pools of conflicted desire, sparkling with unspoken need. "Just don't ask me to stop touching you."

"I don't think I can," she admitted.

I groaned, capturing her lips in a kiss I felt like a fist around the root of my dick.

"I'm going to make you come for me," I told her as I pressed two fingers shallowly into the front wall of her pussy and rubbed while my thumb found the pulsing point of her clit and circled. "I'm going to make you drench these panties in cum until it seeps down your thigh into my lap."

"Rush," she moaned into my mouth, and I ate the sound of my name off her tongue like fucking communion.

It took surprisingly little time to make my innocent church mouse dissolve for me, but when she did, I nearly came in my pants like a fucking teenager. Her entire body went solid, taught with fear as her release loomed over her, threatening to break her open whether she allowed it to or not. For a second, I wondered if she would push me away, stop the slick roll of her hips fucking herself into my hand and close herself off to me.

I looked into her wide eyes as they glazed over, as she froze. Seconds later, she threw her head back on a wild moan and her body quaked until she went boneless. I could feel her cum splash out over my fingers, her thighs squeezing and shaking against my hand. I groaned into her neck, sucking the skin over her pounding pulse to anchor myself to her climax.

Afterward, she drooped into my arms like a ragdoll, her curls in disarray around my shoulders, her hot breath fanning over my neck. I gently removed my fingers from her soaked panties, smoothed them over her swollen sex, and wrapped her as carefully as a fragile present in the cover of my embrace.

It was just a hug, but it nourished my barren soul until those buds bloomed and roots reached deeper.

"Beautiful," I said into her hair as I stroked my hand over it.

She murmured sleepily and nuzzled deeper into my embrace.

I swallowed my laughter and hit the intercom connecting the partitioned back of the car to the driver's seat.

"Buford," I told my driver, confidante, and occasional illegal activity accomplice. "Do we know where Isabella lives?"

"We do, sir. It's an old cottage behind St. Augustine's gardens."

"Take us there."

I sat quietly while we drove, intermittently combing my fingers through Isabelle's ridiculously soft hair. My mind drifted, pleasantly blank, as I absorbed the feel of the trusting, sweet girl in my arms and the delicious fact that she let me play with her untouched pussy.

My phone buzzed with a text.

God: Get your ass over here.

Me: I don't come when called. Not a dog, bro.

God: You come when I call, everyone does.

I snorted as I read his text, because he was not wrong.

God was Baxter Goddard V, the heir to the third largest fortune in the world and the prince of Crescent City.

His father, Four, basically ruled the world, and God thought he did too.

His nickname was more than fitting for his fucking God complex.

Unfortunately, I knew more than most that money could buy you anything.

Like police silence over a suspicious suicide.

God's money had gotten most of the brothers out of their binds over the course of the last few months, and I had no doubt it would get us out of more in the future.

Me: Fine. I'll be there in an hour.

God: Make it thirty minutes.

Me: *middle finger emoji*

"We're here, sir," Buford announced as I tucked my phone back into my pocket.

"Get the doors," I ordered, carefully adjusting Isabelle's heavy, sleeping form in my arms so I could get out of the car.

She muttered something in French, then snuggled into me as I stood with her cradled against my chest. Buford held the door with a curious frown on his face and a smile on his lips.

"Shut up," I told him.

"I didn't say anything, sir."

"Your eyes say it all."

"With all due respect, I'm wearing sunglasses," he pointed out, deadpan.

I grunted as he closed the door and led the way down a small, flower bracketed path to a little, ramshackle cottage.

"Yeah, man, I thought we talked about that. It's fucking midnight, take those things off."

"I have sensitive retinas."

"You wanna look like a badass," I retorted. "Just admit it."

His silence was answer enough, but I stopped ribbing him in order to study the stone house as Buford grabbed the keys from Isabelle's purse.

The inside was only one room, but it was large enough to fit a decent sized bed, full kitchen, and a cordoned off area for the bathroom. There were signs of her personality everywhere, and I sought them out like a fucking bloodhound.

I was right about the knitting. There was a thickly woven cream blanket over the back of the lavender couch, a full basket of paraphernalia on the wicker ottoman, and a half-finished red sweater on the flowery rug. There was a pink tea pot with an empty mug on the bedside table next to a stack of well-read Jane Austen books that spoke of late nights reading and a deeply romantic heart.

SLOTH

As I laid her down on the pale grey sheets and pulled her hair out from under her to splay it over the pillow, I doubted I was the kind of Prince Charming she'd always imagined for herself.

Hell, I was the man who was actually thinking of making a sex tape with her just to complete my task and get to the bottom of the mystery of The Elite.

It had been almost too good to be true when she'd suggested it herself. If I'd been acting normally, smart, and apathetic, like the usual Rush Dempsey, I would have smiled charmingly and towed her to the church to film it right then and fucking there.

But I didn't.

I hesitated like a fucking moron because I liked the way her hair smelled and the look of her pale skin flushed.

I liked the way she settled something restless in my soul while animating factions of it I'd thought were long gone.

She was bringing me back from the living dead and I was helpless to resist.

Feeling like a dipshit because I knew I was going to continue to pursue her even though I'd never be able to give her a simple happily-ever-after, I pressed a kiss to her cheek and got up to leave.

A shadowy figure was standing just outside the open door, leaning against the wall as I went to move past.

I recognized him instantly and felt the hairs on the back of my neck stand on end.

"What the fuck are you doing here?" I barked at the man who had helped wreck each and every one of my brothers' lives.

Standing in the doorway of Isabelle's house, the home

of the woman I'd just silently vowed to have, was not a good fucking omen.

Malcom Benedict stared at me impassively as if I was a bug beneath his shoe. "Good evening, Sloth. I knew you wouldn't be able to resist saving the innocent lamb from the big, bad wolf of Ward Dempsey."

"I asked what the fuck you were doing leaning like a stalker in Isabelle's doorway. Do we have another Dean Griffin situation here?" I accused.

Buford was at my back, waiting silently in the shadows for any indication that Malcom should be put down.

And put him down he would. Buford had been on two tours in Afghanistan and was trained in Krav Maga. He'd been my mother's best friend since their infancy and he'd personally taken it upon himself to be my protector. I'd never asked if it was because my mom had asked him to when I was young, knowing that I was different than my brothers and I needed a guardian, or if it was because Buford sensed something in me that was kin. It didn't matter. We were bonded like the atoms for life.

"I like to keep an eye on all the moving parts as a plan comes together," Malcom said, flicking an invisible piece of lint off his thousand-dollar suit.

"I don't suppose you feel like sharing?" I asked dryly.

"As a matter of fact, I do. Things are coming to a head rather quickly now, but I need you to move things along the way they should."

"What makes you think I'll do anything for you?" I asked, crossing my arms and affecting a casual lean against the wall beside the door after I closed it. "I don't do anything for anyone. If you haven't noticed, I don't give a fuck about much. Besides, you've been my dad's rival for as long as I can remember. The name Malcom is worse than the devil's in the Dempsey house."

"No," he agreed slowly. "But you do give a fuck about finding out what happened to dear old mommy."

My heart calcified in my chest and I forgot how to breathe.

His words simultaneously confirmed I'd been right all along to suspect The Elite had been complicit in her death and that Malcom was more than just a cog in the wheel of the organization.

He was at its apex.

A thin smile curled his lips, reminding me so much of his sister Lillian, I had to supress a shudder of revulsion.

"I thought that would get your attention. I know you've been looking for answers for a long time, boy, and you must be tired of coming up against dead ends. I have a solution for you."

"Why would you help me? You're one of them."

He inclined his head toward me, narrowing his eyes meaningfully. "As are you."

I paused, warring with myself. I wanted whatever information I could get about their role in my mom's death, but I also didn't trust Malcom as far as I could fucking throw him. "Touché. Why don't you tell me what it is you think I want to know, and I'll tell you whether or not you should go straight to hell?"

"Respect," he said in a steely tone, "should be shown at all times in dealings with me if you know what's good for you and yours."

Idly, he knocked his fist against the wall of Isabella's home. I understood his unspoken threat.

I clenched my jaw, but inclined my head.

"Excellent. Now, I'm going to give you vital information, but before I do, you have to understand something. This info is enough to ruin your father. Are you sure you want to do that? You've seemingly changed your tune this past year and turned into a shining example of the Dempsey bloodline. Your daddy is so proud."

"Don't pretend you aren't the wizard of fucking Oz hiding behind a curtain of power and wealth. You know I don't give a fuck if my father lives or dies, let alone if he goes to prison."

"Music to my ears," Malcom said with a grim smile. "Then I'll tell you this. There's a book that contains all the secrets and tasks of The Elite in one leather bound place. It's kept vaulted in one of our leading members' inner sanctuary and you have the key to unlock it."

My brain whirled as I thought about his cryptic words, but the puzzle was easier to solve than it should have been.

"It's at Four's house, isn't it?" I guessed, seeing the glimmer of satisfaction in Malcom's eyes. "God can get it."

"He could. Whether or not he will is another thing, but I've heard you have your father's powers of subtle persuasion."

"Why would you tell me that?" I questioned, even though the new insight was like alcohol on the bonfire of my passion to eradicate The Elite. "What's the catch?"

If we could just get the book...

But then, I knew it was a trap. No member of The Elite would so willingly had over incriminating evidence without wanting something in turn.

This was how power worked, a yin and yang of manipulation and blackmail.

"There's no catch. I just want a look at the book before I hand it over to you for good. And believe me, I'll know if you've looked at it before I've had my chance to."

"That's it?" I asked, suspicion so thick in my blood, it felt like poison.

Malcom's eyes shone as he stepped closer into the light of the lantern over Isabelle's front door.

"I wonder if you've heard I'm running for Senate? I'm not a man that loses—*ever*. And the only way to ensure a win is to take out the obstacles."

I stared after him as he turned, walked back down the path to the waiting Range Rover, and disappeared into the night.

"That man is not your friend," Buford said quietly from behind me.

"No one ever is. That doesn't mean they can't be used. If Malcom wants to destroy my father and the rest of The Elite, let him. Why take them on myself when I can get someone else to do the legwork?"

UINCENDUM NATUS

EIGHT

Rush

I told God about the book that night, but I didn't mention Malcom. He was a shadowy figure in my brothers' lives and they were too focused on the Lillian problem to distract them with thoughts of more. He agreed to get the book even though he was so high on amphetamines, I wasn't sure he'd remember his promise to do so in the morning. His task had fucked him up royally, and to make matters worse, he was half in love with the girl he'd cracked open with his stolen car. After getting belligerently drunk, he told us he was going to Zemira's house. Instead of letting him drive his Ferrari into another car crash, I had Buford take us there.

I'd stand by God, just as I stood by the others while he went through his shit, but this time, I needed something in return from him. I needed that fucking book.

It was one of my first good leads in a year, and I was practically salivating at the idea of getting that dirty diary in my hands.

After leaving God and the guys at his place, I spent the rest of the night having Buford drive me to Baton Rouge to pursue my second lead.

Driving through the gates of the gothic-looking mental hospital gave me hella bad vibes, but I knew it held the answers, and the person, I sought.

I'd never seen Envy the way he was in that hospital. He'd been a decent looking dude before his mind had cracked open, but the combination of a mental break and a shitload of drugs in his system made him look like a half-eaten zombie sitting there on his single bed in the small, white room.

It was depressing as fuck to see him like that, but for one of the first times since Isabelle entered my life, I swallowed down my empathy. I wasn't there to break him out or offer him solace. I was there for answers.

"Hey, brother," I said quietly from the doorway, unsure how he'd react to having me there.

He had been in this place for weeks according to Harriet, and from the look of it, the drugs had gotten the best of him.

What the hell kind of medication did they have him on?

"Micah?" he asked, as if he had spotted his messiah.

I hesitated, but Envy and I had never been particularly close. If he wanted me to be Micah, I could do that.

I stepped into the room and nodded. "Yeah, bro, it's me."

Sebastian almost took me off my fucking feet as he lunged forward and threw his arms around me. I froze, wondering if he was going to attack me or not, then settled when his hoarse voice said in my ear, "It's good to see someone from the outside."

I patted him perfunctorily on the back, but I didn't want him touching me. Hell, I didn't even want to be in the same room as him if I could confirm what he'd done.

"Yeah, I bet. With Sabella still missing, you must be going crazy without answers in here," I said, and immediately felt his body solidify against mine.

I disengaged with him slowly, then took him by the shoulder to lead him to the bed so he could sit down.

"Brother, is there something you want to tell me?" I asked carefully, casually leaning against the wall to give him some space.

"Why did you come to see me, Micah?" he slurred slightly, suspicion heavy in his voice.

I shrugged as if it didn't matter. "You want me to bullshit, or you want me to tell you the truth?"

"The truth," he said, but there was no conviction behind it.

He wasn't even looking at me, his glazed eyes peering into the corner of the room as if it held all the answers to his existence.

"The truth? Funny you should say that because that's exactly why I came to visit you."

My words triggered something in his broken brain. He went rigid, staring into the corner as if a ghost had appeared.

With his next words, I knew the ghost was Sabella.

"I didn't mean to take it that far," he almost whimpered.

SLOTH

There was no one in the room but himself and his demons. Shivers rippled up and down my skin, but I stayed stock still in case I spooked him.

"Why?" I asked quietly.

"Because I envied her. Them. *Everyone*. I just wanted her to be mine, and then she was gone."

Fuck.

Rage surged through me, dormant for so long in my potentially volcanic soul, the sheer heat of the lava swelling in my throat threatened to overtake my mind and body. But I knew instinctively it was exactly that rage that had gotten Wrath arrested for beating up the dean, and it was exactly that capitulation to darkness that had conquered Envy. Maybe it started with giving in just once or twice, but now, he was nothing but a broken shell of a man consumed by anger, jealousy, and crippling regret.

I wouldn't kill him.

At least, not there, not yet.

It was stupid, for one. I'd signed in at the front desk and there was footage of me in their cameras. I wasn't going to jail for anyone, let alone fucking Envy.

But I'd figure out how to make the fucker pay.

Just like I'd make the rest of them.

I turned on my heel without another word and watched as the nurse closed the door with a resounding clang of locks engaging behind me.

She turned to me with a sweet smile. "I hope you enjoyed your visit. I was surprised you were allowed in. Usually his guardian doesn't allow visitors."

"His guardian?" I questioned, carefully modulating my voice so she wouldn't know how hard my heart was pounding. "Right, and that is?"

She frowned at me. "Why, Mr. Benedict, of course."

"Of course," I said smoothly, smiling my Dempsey Ken doll smile at her. "Your lovely face must have distracted me for a minute. What did you say your name was?"

She smiled and tucked her hair behind her ear coquettishly. "Nori."

"Well, Nori, I'll be seeing you again soon. And next time, I'll be bringing my brothers."

I was just pulling up to the colossal wrought iron gates of the Dempsey compound when my phone buzzed. At first, I was tempted to ignore it. It seemed like all I did these days was rush to the aid of my fellow Elite brothers, but I'd been up all damn night getting to Baton Rouge and back and figured I deserved a break.

Only, I'd texted Isabelle earlier and hadn't heard back. A part of me didn't expect to. She was a good girl and had come to her senses, maybe even thought shacking up with my bastard of a father was a comfortable idea, if not the best one.

So, I looked.

Church Mouse: They know.

A portentous chill swept through my body as Buford opened the door for me and I stepped up to the massive double doors. I looked down at my leather boots resting on the doormat that read DEMPSEY and ground my heel into the fabric.

I knew what she meant by her cryptic text.

Somehow, our fathers had found out about last night.

It explained why I'd been summoned home to speak with my father, but it didn't explain what Archbishop Savoie might do to Isabelle for her transgressions.

SLOTH

Gritting my teeth, I pushed through the doors without knocking, crossed the marble foyer, ignoring our butler, Jackson, and stormed into my father's office.

I stood in the entrance, my chest heaving with rage, my hands clenched by my side, but my voice was crushed under the iron grip of wrath around my throat.

Since I'd joined The Elite, I'd experienced more of the deadly sins than I ever had in my entire life.

The increasing itch of emotions colliding and reforming like newly formed atoms under my skin made my entire body feel agitated and ill at ease. I was raised to be cold, factual, and oblivious to the needs of others by the very best example of all three characteristics.

I stared at him, then across the large expanse of his office, and thought for the millionth time people were too quick to underestimate the idle and wealthy. More often than not, it was they who did the devil's best work.

Ward Dempsey was not a flashy man. He had the laminated good looks of the wealthy and well-bred, as well as the manners and reserve to go along with them, but there was nothing threatening or gregarious about his person. He looked very much like a political Ken doll seated in his leather, tufted chair behind his palatial desk in a room with walls covered in books.

But his mediated pleasantness was exactly what made my father so powerful.

He worked best in the shadows at the back of the room, where the assistans, vice presidents, and COOs stood. It was there, posed as a like-monded wallflower, that he whispered his masterful manipulations into the right ears like a farmer sowing his fields.

He stared at me over the steeple of his fingers, a

habitual posture that was laughable because it gave him the illusion of prayer.

My father was not a religious man.

He believed in no God but himself, no faith but that of The Elite.

"Once again, Rush, you've proven to be a disappointment to this family," he began in a modulated tone, as if he was a professor reading out from a text. "Your actions on behalf of the Dempsey name are inexcusable. How do you dare to defend yourself?"

I didn't want to dare.

This was why I avoided going home at all costs. My three older brothers were carbon copies of my father, and they too thought I was a piece of shit unworthy of the Dempsey name. No amount of defending myself could change that fact.

But I'd been called to judgement by the head of the family and knew he wouldn't let me leave until I said my piece.

"You couldn't have been serious about marrying a twenty-four-year-old girl like Isabelle Savoie anyway," I said, perching on the edge of the chair before his desk, my hands in my pockets.

It was an irreverent posture that made my father glower at me.

"I was absolutely serious. Candidates with spouses do better in the polls. I've been a widow for a year, which is the appropriate amount of time before I take a new wife. Isabelle's purity and connections to the church were exactly what I needed for my platform. It will be an edge over that conceited prick Malcom Benedict who is notoriously single. You've tried to ruin that for me."

"How was I supposed to know you'd go for a girl closer to my age than yours?" I asked with a shrug. "Didn't know dear old daddy was a cradle robber among your other list of crimes."

"Here we go again," Ward said meanly. "You want to bring up accusations that I was at the root of your mother's *suicide*?"

"Nothing you say will convince me otherwise," I told him calmly. "You and The Elite ruined her."

"She ruined herself. It's not either of our faults she was too weak to live with the responsibilities of great power. If you're not careful, Rush," he practically purred, "you'll go the same way."

"You mean you and The Elite will kill me for asking the wrong questions?" I retorted.

My dad only smiled and I realized it was the same smile I'd seen on Malcom Benedict's face, an expression that was more a thinly veiled threat than an example of mirth.

"Isabelle won't marry you," I said, pulling the fat joint from behind my ear and twirling it lazily between my fingers because my father hated that I blazed.

"She will. Unlike me with you, her father hasn't failed to take her in hand. He'll make her marry me, and I expect you to let it happen. You have a terrible habit of chasing after things you'll never achieve while ignoring other, more important goals. Is it any wonder they gave you the sin of Sloth?"

"Is it any wonder they gave you Pride?" I countered. "You think life is a game and people are just pieces on a board, but every time you sacrifice a player, you ruin their lives, Dad. It's a reality, not a construction. Mum is probably just one in a thousand causalities of your crusade to get to the top."

"If that's the truth, boy, don't you think you should be more careful around me?" he asked pleasantly. "Don't you think you should do as I say and pick up the family torch? Levi, Chase, and Harrison are all aligning themselves on paths of power, while you continually try to eviscerate the family name. I'm telling you for the last time, get on the same page as your brothers. I won't let anyone tarnish the family name or my future, not even my own son."

I stared at him, unwilling and unable to understand how a father could so easily threaten his own blood. My mother hadn't been anything like him. She had been magic and kindness, empathy and charity.

He was every kind of demonic creature that lived in the dark places of the human heart.

"Well then, daddy-o," I said as I stood up and flipped my lighter open to light my joint and take a long, much-needed drag, "I guess the gauntlet has been thrown. Let the best man—or the worst man—win."

VII

UINCENDUM NATUS

NINE

Isabelle

"I can't hear you," he roared.

I couldn't hear myself because my ears were ringing, so it was difficult to gage how loudly I should repent.

"I will not disobey," I croaked through my tear ravaged throat, bracing for the blow.

My father's hand connected with cheek like a bomb, sending shards of shrapnel edged pain into the sockets behind my eyes, the soft spots at my temples, and the base of my skull. My entire head rang with pain, but I only had one more slap before I would be absolved of my sins.

At least, physically. I knew there would be more punishment after that. My father's God called for atonement in the flesh, spirit, and mind of a sinner.

"I will obey my Heavenly Father and worldly father in all ways," I yelled through the pain.

The last blow fell hard against my right cheekbone, my father's state championship football ring slicing through the skin like a warm knife through butter.

My head fell between my shoulders where I kneeled, braced against the statue of Virgin Mary on the altar of St. Augustine's Cathedral. Warm blood ran down my cheek and dripped, dripped to the floor.

I could see him cleaning his hands on a handkerchief in my blurry peripheral, and I knew the worst had passed.

He always felt better after taking his hands to me.

The only way to chase the devil out of a born sinner like me was to beat it out.

He'd been telling me that since I was a girl when my mother left us to return to her native France. Her leaving was my fault. I was a sinner and my mother was embarrassed of me. If I wanted to grow up to be a good girl and then a good woman, I would have to obey my father and let him lead me into the light so I could eventually go to Heaven.

It started with spankings, a ruler or his hand. He only began to hit me when I entered puberty.

Deep in my soul, I knew my father was using God's voice as a tool against me, just as he used his fists, but it was only in the last few years I'd allowed that knowledge to grow and bloom in my mind.

He didn't like women.

He ignored his female disciples if he could and lauded the men for their faithfulness. He kept only choir boys and male staff, and he made me wear frumpy, old lady clothing because it stripped me of my femininity.

SLOTH

He was a beast of hell dressed in the robes of the Lord.

For the first time in my life as I knelt there bleeding, the taste of Rush Dempsey still on the back of my tongue, I allowed myself to hate my father.

"You will clean the cathedral until it sparkles, then go without food for three days, Isabelle," my father ordered, his voice flaccid now that he'd spent his hatred on me.

"Yes, Father," I agreed.

"You know, they asked for you at the nunnery, and I would have been well within my rights to send you there, but I decided you'd be more useful here with me. Don't make me regret that decision."

There was blood in my hair and my bangs were plastered to my forehead with sweat. I read once that sweat smelled different depending on the reason for it. The perspiration born from fear was the strongest, most acidic stench.

I reeked of it and the metallic tang of bloody despair.

"In the future, when I tell you to do something, I expect you to do it without question. Ward Dempsey is a very important man in The Elite, I—no—*we* owe our lives to him, do you understand? If he wants you to perk up his campaign, I will hand you over on a silver platter. Now, we'll have to wait days before he can take you out in public. You aren't presentable in your current condition."

Because you beat me, the growing voice of strength and independence in my soul screamed out.

Still, I was smart enough, diligent enough, not to cave into such a base rage. I waited until the sound of his feet on the marble receded into nothingness, then I began to clean.

I swept and waxed the floor, oiled the wooden pews, dusted the pulpit, and scrolled woodwork bracketing the organ, but I kept the bloody altar for last.

As I knelt on sore knees to stare at the puddle of my blood at Mary's feet, the doors at the front of cathedral opened and the fierce gale of a spring storm swept through, cleansing the room and swirling deliciously around my hot, sticky flesh.

I remained on the altar, hoping the low lights we kept on after hours were dim enough to conceal my form bent on the ground.

The sound of heavy footsteps rang out through the hollow chamber, closer and closer, until they stopped at my back.

Still, I didn't move, but not because I was afraid.

I knew with a sense I attributed to my God and not my father's false one, the man at my back was more protector than punisher.

The ultimate friend instead of the usual foe.

Soft as a butterfly, a hand skimmed over the back of my sweat-matted hair, moving the length of it to one side of my neck. Tenderly, fingers traced the shape of my ear and spilled down the line of my neck.

I held my breath as a soft thud sounded behind me. He knelt at my back and carefully wound his arms around my torso to hug me against his strong body.

Instantly, tears I hadn't even been conscious of harboring swept down my cheeks and neck onto his lean forearms.

"Darlin'," he cooed into the hair over my ear before he pressed a kiss there. "Please tell me that isn't your blood on the altar."

I tried three times to speak before my throat made a sound. "I can't."

Rush's fury blazed like a sudden inferno around us, but I felt safe from the flames tucked close to his body in his gentle embrace.

His anger was righteous, his desire for revenge just.

If someone had hurt him the same way, I knew I would feel exactly what he felt then.

He was silent for a long time, breathing in long, controlled pulls of air to calm the heartbeat I felt pounding against my shoulders.

"I'm okay," I told him weakly, knowing it was a bandage on an open wound.

"No, you aren't," he whispered fiercely. "But you will be."

I resisted when he tried to turn my face so he could see the damage. "No, please, I don't want you to see me like this. I think...I think maybe you'll kill him if you do."

A shudder of impotent wrath rolled through him.

"Fine. Are you okay to make your way back to the cottage to collect your things?"

"Why?"

"Because there is no way in hell I'm letting you stay within walking distance of your motherfucking father," he growled.

"Rush, please, we're in the house of the Lord," I reprimanded without conviction.

I didn't want to stay within walking distance of my father either.

Not walking, running, or driving distance.

I wanted him below the crust of the earth where only the worst kinds of demons raged.

"I can get my stuff," I said.

Rush pressed a long, soft kiss to my pulse point and gently constricted his arms around me. "Pack everything you care about. I don't expect you to be back here until the end."

"What end?"

"The end of The Elite," he said ominously before standing and helping me up.

He was careful not to look at my face as I turned to make my way out the side door down the path to my little house. I knew it was because he planned to face my father before taking me away for good.

I only prayed, of the two sinners, the right man would win.

VII

UINCENDUM NATUS

TEN

Rush

As I stalked through the cold, eerie halls of St. Augustine's Cathedral, I tried to control the masses of adrenaline surging through my body. I'd never felt so energized with purpose, so filled to the brim with absolute conviction.

I wasn't sure I liked the feeling.

I thought I might be having a heart attack.

But as the door to the archbishop's office loomed ahead of me, I knew I'd take a fucking heart attack as penance so long as I could beat the shit out of him for taking a hand to Isabelle before I died.

I pushed open the door to see the sorry excuse for a religious zealot sitting at his desk clipping his fingernails.

For some reason, the mundane image infuriated me.

How could a man beat his daughter, then do something so innocuous, as if it was just another day in the life?

He looked up at me with a frown, obviously not recognizing me as a Dempsey even though I was almost the spitting image of my father. "It's after hours, young man. If you need confession, please come back tomorrow at eight."

"I think it's you who needs confession," I told him, calmly rolling up the sleeves of my dress shirt. "I wasn't aware Catholics believed in physical acts of repentance."

His vaguely irritated frown turned black with hatred. "Everyone's practices are different, but here, in this church and this city, my word is God."

"Funny you should say that. I know another God, and as crazy as he can be sometimes, I think he's got more authority on the matter of goodness than you do."

"Your opinion is irrelevant. St. Augustine and Isabelle are mine to rule as I please," he seethed, his face turning red with rage. "Who are you to stroll in here and doubt *me*?"

"I'm Rush fucking Dempsey," I said, just to watch his jaw drop open.

"Your father will not be happy to hear his son is sticking his nose places it does not belong," he threatened.

I laughed. "My father hasn't been happy with me my entire life. At least this time, I'm doing something worthy of his criticism."

"And what is it exactly you think you're doing?" Archbishop Savoie sneered at me. "You're just a boy with no power, trying to play knight-in-shining-armor for a woman you can't have. This is how it's going to go, I'll pretend this disrespectful incident never happened and you'll crawl back home with your tail between your legs to apologize to your father for almost derailing our plans. Then, I expect to see you at Sunday sermon to pray for my and the Holy Father's forgiveness."

"I'm not my father. I don't give a fuck about what you, he, or anyone else thinks. And I'm not so good at following orders," I said, cracking my knuckles and my rolling my head between my shoulders. "So, let *me* tell *you* how this is going to go."

Slowly, I stalked over to him, watching as he realized I was a bodily threat to him. He was a big man, but his muscles were layered with fat. My youth and vigor would make me victorious if he wanted a real fight.

Personally, I yearned for it. If the motherfucker fought back, I'd have even more reason to pummel his thick face.

"Now, I'm going to give you a little sermon, motherfucker," I said as I braced myself on either arm of his chair, caging him in. "I'm not usually a very impassioned guy, but when I see a fucking grown man taking his fists to a slip of a girl, a girl who is everything good and kind, it makes me want to get my hands a little dirty. And you know what I want to dirty them with? Your blood."

He opened his mouth, rage in his eyes as he tried to get out of his chair. Instead, I pinned him to the high-backed cushion with one hand and sent my other fist crashing down on his meaty nose.

I felt the bones break under my hand, crunching like blown glass into splinters and shards. Blood exploded from the gash I made with my signet ring in his flesh and poured from his nostrils down the front of his red robes.

"You're a piece of shit wrapped in the cloth of a God who wouldn't even accept you into Heaven for what you've done to your daughter," I said calmly into his face, harnessing his flailing hands by the wrists with each of my own.

He was strong, but he was cornered prey to the predator inside me I'd finally let out to play.

"I'm taking Isabelle away with me. If you come looking for her, if you lay another hand on her, I'll turn you into a fucking eunuch. Is that clear?"

"You don't know who you're dealing with," he spat out, blood flying over the front of my white shirt. "We will end you, boy."

I let the rage that had been percolating in my heart since my mother's death rush to the surface of my expression, twisting it into a mask of hatred. "I know exactly who you are and who you think will protect you. It's about time you fuckers got the message—and you might as well be the messenger." I leaned in so my eyes were all he could see and ground the heel of my hand into his messed-up nose until he shouted in agony. "My brothers and I are coming for you."

VII

UINCENDUM NATUS

ELEVEN

Isabelle

R ush had been quiet the entire car ride, and the silence was starting to wear on my frayed nerves. He'd taken one look at my cut and swollen face before the shutters crashed down over his expression and the usual, implacable, without-a-care Rush Dempsey took control. I noticed the blood on his hands as he helped me into the car, then carefully tucked me under his arm to snuggle into his warm side, but I didn't comment on it. I knew the blood was my father's, but instead of castigating him for resorting to violence, I felt a dark thrill knowing he'd extracted an almost medieval vengeance from my father for his misdeeds.

I watched as Rush's phone buzzed with a multitude of incoming texts and peeked over his shoulder to see him texting with a series of people named after the seven deadly sins.

"Who is that?" I asked, my curiosity getting the better of me.

He pressed a kiss to my head and resumed stroking my hair.

He didn't even say anything as Buford helped me out of the car and Rush rounded the side to escort me through the gate of a classic New Orleans Greek revival style home. There was a wrought iron, scroll work railing around both the first and second story porches, two white columns in the front, and a door painted a sinful red.

It was the most beautiful home I'd ever seen, and my father had a huge mansion in uptown. There was just something storybook about the home that made me feel like it was the setting of a happily-ever-after.

I snuck a peek at Rush as he opened the door with a passcode, wondering if maybe it could be the setting of *our* happily-ever-after.

He frowned at me as he caught sight of the damage to my face again, then carefully smoothed out his features as he led me into the cool, high-ceiling foyer.

I twisted my hands together, desperate for his comfort, both physically and verbally. It was strange and unsettling to realize I was needy for both after knowing him for only a few weeks. For a moment, I wondered if I only wanted one to replace one man's influence in my life with another. I wondered if I was meek and incapable of dictating my own destiny.

The thought faded quickly.

I was the best student in my Master program's graduating class that year while also acting as St. Augustine cathedral's administrative assistant. I wasn't a genius, I didn't have any friends my age unless you counted a few of my father's flock, but I had indominable work ethic and knew that would carry me forward to success in my life no matter the setbacks.

"Why don't you take a shower?" Rush interrupted my thoughts to offer.

I blinked at my surroundings, realizing he had led us into the back of the house to a large, masculine master suite.

He stared at me without expression, his eyes hooded so low, I couldn't read the thoughts in his dark eyes. I wanted to beg him to talk to me, to crack open the turmoil of whatever emotions were slowly eating away at his soul so I could soothe them, but I didn't have the confidence to do so.

Instead, I nodded and walked into the big, black-tiled bathroom. When I turned around to close the door, it was already clicking shut, Rush's booted footsteps fading farther into the house.

I let out a gusty breath and turned to examine the damage in the bathroom mirror.

My left cheekbone was swollen, a deep, short gash splitting the skin like an overripe tomato. Tears had cut tracks through the blood, and my hair had matted into sweaty, bloody chunks.

I looked like I'd been dredged up from the bowls of hell.

As I turned on the rainfall shower and shed my ugly, shapeless clothes to step under the hot spray, I felt the keen edge of regret slice through what remained of my composure.

Rush had just saved me.

The man I had called 'the worst kind of fornicator' had just stood up to my father and installed me in his home so I could be safe and comfortable.

He'd taken me on when all I presented to him was time and effort, two things I thought he abhorred.

And I'd unfairly judged him because my father's God had told me there were only two types of people: sinners and saints.

Rush was both and neither.

He was kind, but uneasily moved, just, but brutal in his retaliation, handsome, but sinfully so. He was an enigma wrapped in pretty paper and tied with a lazy bow.

I wanted to spend time unveiling him because something told me, even though I'd judged him as the worst kind of man, he was best one I knew.

When I stepped out of the shower, my body scrubbed so clean my skin glowed pink and fresh, I wrapped myself in a towel and vowed to thank him from the bottom of my heart and to apologize for my gross error in judgement.

I opened the bathroom to look for him, and the soft swell of piano music swept over me. I recognized the song instantly as Jeff Buckley's "Hallelujah."

Following the sound, I padded barefoot through the big house to the front room where I froze in the doorway so I wouldn't disturb him.

Rush was at a gorgeous antique grand piano, his gold hair falling over his face as his hands moved languidly against the keys.

My breath caught in my throat at the sight of him lost to the music, smoke from a lit marijuana cigarette perched on an ashtray beside him curling over his head like a dirty halo. I'd never seen someone so beautiful in my life.

Sensing me, he lifted his head and stared at me from under low lids, his gaze raking over every inch of my towel-covered form. There was nothing in his face to give away his desire, but I sensed it in the air between us as it turned electric like the sky before a summer storm.

I wanted him too.

Not because I wanted to be corrupted to avoid a strange arrangement with Ward or to cut ties for good with my father, but because my body wanted him and my spirit yearned to be joined with his.

There was something about the bad boy across from me that called out to my soul.

I just had to be brave enough to call back to his.

Sucking in a deep breath, I took a step forward and let the towel drop to the ground.

Rose gold light from the setting sun spilled into the room and across Rush's face, turning his dark eyes to burning coals.

"I'm not going to touch you," he said as he continued to play. "Not after what happened to you today."

"I want you to," I said, my heart lodged in my throat.

"I'm not going to take advantage of you when you're clearly vulnerable." His eyes slid away from my naked body as if it was nothing. "I left clothes out for you on the bed. Get changed and we'll order in some food."

"Rush," I called out, somewhat desperately before all my confidence evaporated in the vacuum of his disregard. "Please, touch me. I want your body to cover my scars and your hands to soothe them with your touch. I want your lips to heal the wounds I wear on my heart and your eyes to ignore the ones marring my face. I want you to show me what it's like to love another body with your own."

The music drifted to nothing as he stared at his still hands on the keys. Finally, his composure had cracked like a fissure down the middle of his face. When he looked up at me again, his features were soft with awe and flushed with passion.

My heart beat savagely in my throat as he slowly stood up and prowled across the room to me. I gasped as he moved into me, gently but firmly taking me into his arms with his hands under my bottom as he continued to walk from the room.

"I don't know how to love," he admitted hoarsely. "But I'll show you worship."

I wrapped my arms around his neck to hold on and twined my fingers in the short hair at the back of his neck. I wanted to tell him I knew about love and could show him the way to my heart if he wanted to take it, but I was too mired in the depths of his gorgeous brown eyes to re-member my voice.

When we reached his bedroom, he laid us down gen-tly on the bed, his big, lean body between my thighs. He stroked my hair away from my face, and said, "Tell me if you need me to stop. I don't want to hurt you."

"My face is fine."

One of his hands smoothed down my neck, between my small breasts, over my belly, and between my legs where he shamelessly cupped my sex.

"It will hurt here when I take you," he told me before pressing a kiss to my sternum. "But only for a minute."

I scratched at his shoulders to bring his face back to

mine, then kissed him, sweeping my tongue past his full lips to touch it to his.

"I want the pleasure and the pain," I whispered against his mouth, feeling him shudder at my words.

"Fuck, you're so sexy," he groaned.

The words trilled through me like a birdsong.

I'd never been sexy in my life. It felt powerful, forbidden.

I tightened my hands in his hair and brought his mouth back to mine for another toe-curling kiss.

From there, Rush took control, kissing me until my mind spun, playing with my increasingly wet pussy until I bloomed under his touch, open and supple for his stretching fingers.

I groaned in protest when he rolled to his side away from me, but he only smiled languidly. "Climb up here."

I frowned at him in confusion, then squeaked when he clasped my hips in his big hands and dragged me over and up his body so I straddled his face.

"Rush," I protested, struggling to climb off him. "This is...no, it's—" My words ended in a strangled moan as his mouth opened under me and closed over my aching clit.

I squirmed as his arms strapped over my thighs, unsure if I was still trying to flee or attempting to grind down farther on his plundering tongue. The feel of his lips against my most intimate flesh was heavenly. I could feel myself grow slick and swollen, my nerve-endings firing into sparks and threatening to turn into fireworks.

"Rush, ah, oh my..." I moaned thoughtlessly, consumed by the glory of his mouth on me.

"That's right, darlin', come all over my tongue," he encouraged me, speaking against my shamefully damp inner thigh before nipping at the flesh in a way that made my sex spasm. "I could spend all day eating at your sweet, pink pussy."

His words tied me into knots, his mouth pulling the threads so taut, I almost couldn't breathe. Then, just when I thought I couldn't take it anymore, he slid a finger inside me to rub at my front wall.

I tore apart with pleasure, every knot in my muscles snapping tight then ripping away so I fell lax against the headboard breathing hard, still gyrating lightly onto Rush's sweetly lapping tongue as he licked up my cum.

I rested my forehead against my headboard as I caught my breath. To my surprise, I didn't feel ashamed or dirty after so brazenly riding his face.

If anything, I felt further enflamed.

I pushed off the headboard to scoot down Rush's body, settling my hips over his tummy because I was too afraid to straddle the enormous erection I felt at my back. I leaned over his chest, loving the feel of his light chest hair against my nipples, his strong abs under my belly. I played my fingers in the ends of his hair and brushed one thumb over his swollen, glistening lower lip.

"Do I taste good?" I asked hesitantly, staring at the wetness on my thumb.

His hands found my hips and squeezed even as his eyes dared me. "Why don't you see for yourself?"

I bent closer, tentatively moving my mouth over his before he took control of the kiss and slid his tongue into my mouth.

He tasted warm, clean, and wet, maybe slightly salty. I moaned at the wickedness of licking myself out of his mouth, and he groaned in answer, sliding me farther down his torso so his erection was sandwiched between my wet legs and his stomach.

"You taste like silk and sunshine," he told me, smacking a kiss against my lips and a hand lightly against my clit. "Here *and* here."

My skin flushed like a burn. "Rush!"

His eyes sparkled with playfulness. "I like telling you what to do, how well you do it, and how good you taste. It turns me on to watch my words affect you like this. Look at how your nipples harden and your eyes darken when I talk dirty to my pure girl."

I decided to shut him up with a kiss, smiling into his mouth as he laughed huskily into mine. I'd never known sex could be fun and light-hearted, easy and sexy.

"Now," he said as he twined a hand in my hair and gently, but firmly, tugged on it so I was forced up and away from him. "I want you to be my good girl and sit yourself down on my cock just like I told you I wanted you to do in the Rolls."

I squirmed, inadvertently sliding myself up and down his dick in a way that had us both panting. "Can't you... um, do it?"

"No," he told me sternly, his eyes hooded and cheeks streaked with a high flush. He looked like a sex God lounging back on the pillow, waiting for a nymph to service him. "I'll tell you what to do, but you're going to fuck me tonight, Isabelle."

A delicious thrill sluiced through my body at the thought. I bit my lip as I splayed my hands over his chest, then ran them down his rippling torso. "Where do I start?"

"Wrap your hand around my big dick," he coached,

linking his hands behind his head in a position that was both arrogant and ridiculously sexy.

I lifted my hips so I could expose his erection, then allowed myself to feast my eyes on his impossible length. It jumped, the veins pulsing as I wrapped my fingers around it one by one until my index and thumb nearly touched in a vice around his flesh. The shaft was dusky red silk over steel. Instinctively, I flexed my hand around him and heard his sharp intake of breath as his dick twitched.

"That's it. Do you see the drop of pre-cum at the tip? Rub your thumb over that, then in a circle over the head of my cock," he instructed hoarsely, watching from narrowed eyes as I followed his orders.

The pre-cum was slick, his cock burning hot under my ministrations. I tucked my tongue between my teeth in concentration, then thought, "What does that taste like?"

Before he could say anything, I ducked down to swipe my tongue over the tip. Salty, musky sweetness exploded in my mouth.

Rush's muscular thighs were taught, his abs contracted in an effort to stay still for me.

I looked up through my lashes at him, and said, "You taste even better than me."

"Jesus Christ," he swore thickly, the tendons in his neck straining. "I need to feel your tight pussy around me. Do you think you're ready for me?"

I stared at the long appendage in my hand. "You're awfully big."

"You don't have to," he reminded me, even though I could feel his legs quake as I rubbed my thumb over his wet head again and again. "We can stop now."

"No," I said firmly, echoing his early rebuttal. "I want you inside me."

I adjusted my position, angling his dick so it notched against my entrance.

"Look at me," he ordered.

Our eyes clanged as they locked together, both of us panting as I paused.

"Sink onto me until you can't anymore, then I'll take over."

I lowered myself until his flesh parted my folds and sunk inside my wet heat. We both moaned at the sensation. I tried to go farther, but a pinching sensation made me pause.

Rush reached for me, wrapping my torso in his arms so I was bent over him again, our foreheads pressed together and mouths open against one another.

"I could worship you like this forever," he vowed, before punching his hips against mine in a movement that seared through me like fire.

He sealed his lips over mine, eating my cries off over my tongue, soothing me with a hand stroking down my back. My body tensed over him, fighting the invasion.

"Relax for me, darlin'," Rush rasped against my mouth before sucking kisses onto my neck in a way that made me dizzy. "Sit down on my cock and take it like my good, sweet girl."

His words unlocked the tension in my muscles. I automatically sunk down flush against his groin. I squirmed slightly, then again, finding his coarse, short pubic hair felt good against my swollen clit.

"Play with your pussy for me," he ordered softly as he braced himself on an elbow to push me into a sitting position on top of him. "Play with your clit and move on my cock until it feels good for you. Use me to make yourself cum."

I moved my hips, letting my instincts guide me. His cock felt thick as a fist inside me, rubbing against every surface of my pussy as I moved forward and back, up and down. I went faster, catching a primal rhythm that had my breasts bouncing and my head thrown back to moan.

"Fucking gorgeous," Rush groaned as I moved and moved. "You look like a goddess riding me like that, taking your pleasure from me like it's your right."

The heat between my legs built, kindled by the filth coming out of his mouth and his big cock thrusting between my legs, but it wasn't enough to set me fully ablaze.

"Play with your nipple," Rush barked, his voice strained with passion. "Harder than that. Pull and twist them until they're rose red for me."

"I need…" I whimpered, so close to the edge, it felt like vertigo.

"I know what you need, darlin'," he growled before rearing up so I flipped onto my back and my legs surged into the air on either side of him.

He captured them on his shoulder, then pinned me open with his torso as he leaned in to tug on my nipple brutally and kiss me like a savage.

"This is what you need, isn't it?" he asked, an edge of harshness to his voice. "I can worship you with my body, hard or soft, and my girl wants it hard."

He was right.

Seconds after he started pounding into me, the wet slap of our flesh and the rough edge of our groans heightening the turmoil of sensations in my body, I caught fire.

Flames licked over my hips, thighs, sex, and belly, lighting in my painfully hard nipple as he pulled at them and sinking deep under every inch of flesh he touched. I felt razed like a phoenix to ashes. As Rush shouted out his orgasm, his dick pulsing inside me as he came, I knew our act would be just as restorative.

I closed my eyes as he slumped beside me. He was careful not to crush me, but kept me close with his arms and a leg thrown over my thighs. I listened to his heavy breath and focused on the way his thumb caressed the bottom of one of my breasts.

It felt like I was in my own personal heaven on earth.

I opened my eyes and turned my head to stare at the angel who'd taken me there with him.

He had these heavy lidded, almond-shaped eyes that always seemed slumberous and indolently sexy, like he'd woken from a post-coital nap. They were closed as he recovered, but even then, I remembered the way they'd felt against my skin as I rode him. I ran my fingers over his eyelashes, and they fluttered under my touch, thick and soft as a mink pelt. When they opened, his big brown eyes drowned me in heat, hot coffee against my skin, sliding down my throat to warm my insides, sluicing across my skin until I was scalded with third degree burns I'd live with under my flesh for the rest of my life.

"How do you feel?" he asked softly.

"Thoroughly corrupted," I said with a smile.

"Most people call me lazy, but you know the old saying?" he asked, pressing his smile into my hair. "'The devil finds work for idle hands to do.'"

I laughed, but then I noticed the somber cast to his features and wondered if he actually thought he'd done me a disservice by taking my virginity even though I'd practically begged him to.

"They also say the devil can live inside a person," I whispered in the air between us. I pressed my palm on top of his against the vulnerable valley over my blasphemous heart. "You're truth of that."

Rush closed his eyes tight against the flood of feeling that contorted his features. "I'm not used to this."

"What? Needy ex-virgins in your bed?" I teased self-consciously.

"No, feeling so much."

My heart panged for him. I flipped over onto my stomach to prop one arm on the bed and another on his chest so I could take my chin in my hands as I looked down at him. Now that we'd shared the ultimate intimacy, I found I didn't want to give up the privilege of touching him.

"Will you tell me something?" I asked.

"Like what?"

"Something no one else knows," I gambled on asking.

I wanted to know him with a desperation that bordered on zealousness. It was as if I was replacing my enthusiasm for Catholicism with another form of religion, one found on discourse between bodies and sermons of the soul.

For a moment, I thought he wouldn't say anything, then his fingers reached up to play with the ends of my curls and his other hand settled on the small of my back as if to anchor me to him.

"I'll tell you something," he started slowly. "I'll tell you a story, but it's not a happy one and it doesn't have an ending yet. Are you sure you want to hear it?"

I nodded. There wasn't a single thing I didn't want to know about him.

He dragged in a deep breath and began. "Three things shaped my life in my first nineteen years of existence…"

I listened to his story with tears in my eyes and bile on the back of my tongue. Even though questions burned in my throat, I didn't interrupt him to ask them. There was a faraway look in his eyes as he told me about Magnolia's death, the abhorrent acts committed by this secret society, The Elite, and the things he and his friends had done to be part of it.

My heart stopped when he admitted in a matter-of-fact voice his task had been to desecrate the church.

To defile me.

My skin went hot, then arctic cold as all the warmth of our love making fled my body through the puncture wound his words inflicted.

I almost didn't notice his next words because they were spoken in the same bored monotone.

"I don't know who gave me the task, only that it had to be a faction of the society because Archbishop Savoie is *in* The Elite and to destroy him would also, somehow, destroy my father. I don't care. I didn't have any intention of fulfilling my task, but I was curious about the girl they'd sent me to defile like a succubus from hell. So, I went to the church."

He blinked slowly. When his gorgeous brown eyes opened again, they were focused, razor sharp with intent, on my face. "I saw you sitting there with rosary beads in your hand and a ribbon in your hair, and I wanted you with a ferocity I've never experienced before."

"So…" I cleared my throat and licked my dry lips,

"two birds one stone? You completed your task and got your rocks off with the little virgin girl?"

His arms tightened around me and the placid expression he'd been wearing turned to stone with conviction. "More like I was handed a poisoned apple and instead of eating it, I went to an apple grove and found paradise."

I hesitated, and his eyes melted like chocolate, sweet and dark on my face.

"I found you, and I'm keeping you. I found you, and I took you, knowing I'd be dragging you into my hellish world and also knowing I'd protect you from it at all fucking costs. Am I making myself clear, darlin'?"

I'd never experienced the kind of love that took a stranglehold of my heart in that moment. I'd once had the warmth of childhood love for my parents and still had the spiritual anchor of love for my God, but I'd never had this love so fierce, it physically hurt my chest to bear it.

As if sensing my pain, Rush placed a kiss to my breastbone before continuing. "It's up to you if you want to be with a solider on crusade. I'm on a mission, and I won't stop until each and every one of those motherfuckers is brought to justice for what they've done. Lillian and George Griffin, Four, Malcom Benedict, Envy...even the nameless who wear their hoods and bear the seal because one or more of the seven deadly sins makes them corrupt for power—I'll kill them if I have to, Isabelle. You have to know that."

I looked into his eyes, the beautiful gaze of a man who looked like a fallen angel with the morals of a sinner and an imperfect human heart.

As I placed a hand on his cheek, I sensed his tension unravel like a spool of thread and wondered with awe how I could have that impact on him.

He trusted me, and in turn, I could do only one thing for him.

"I don't condone murder, but I also can't pretend those...animals don't need to be put down. You saved me from my own monster, so I'm not ignorant to the cruelty of the world and the fact that it often goes disproved. I have faith in you, Rush. I have faith you'll do what needs to be done in the end, and I'll stand by you while you do it."

"No one has ever said that to me before," he admitted on a quiet breath.

"That your mission is righteous?"

"That they have faith in me."

Sorrow wrapped its velvet arms around my soul and made me want to weep. Instead, I kissed Rush with all the compassion in my heart and to delight in distracting us both with my newfound sense of proactiveness.

VII

UINCENDUM NATUS

TWELVE

Isabelle
Two weeks later

I was bent over my textbooks and notebook studying for my midterm exam on 19th century psychologists when there was a sudden tug on the ribbon in my hair and my curls went tumbling around my shoulders.

A second later, warm lips pressed to my ear, and rasped, "I've wanted to do that since the moment I first saw you in St. Augustine's Cathedral."

I giggled at the thought. "You're not serious."

"Deadly," Rush deadpanned before moving my hair to the side so he could softly bite the skin over my pulse. "I also wanted to retie it around your throat so you'd feel it like my hand around your neck every time you breathed."

A shiver danced down my spine even though I looked guiltily around the library at the other students trying to study there.

"Rush, we're in public. You should behave," I scolded lightly.

He chuckled, pulling out the chair beside me so he could flop down into it, a hand still tangled in one side of my hair. "Since when do I care about behaving?"

"You have a point," I admitted.

He laughed, and I noticed he'd been doing that a lot the past few weeks. It was bizarre to think we'd only known each other a short time, and somehow, we were already living together. It was also a little embarrassing to admit how easily I'd taken to living a life of sin with him. Sexually, we couldn't get enough of each other, and each time we had sex, it got just a little bit darker, a little bit less tame.

It should have frightened me, but it didn't.

I welcomed Rush's darkness, and he welcomed my light.

We'd found a strange sense of yin and yang that worked for us.

I was head over heels in love with him, but I hadn't said the words because I remembered all too clearly what he had said the night he took my virginity.

I don't know how to love.

I intended to show him every day until he did, but until then, I was happy.

Or as happy as I could be when Rush ducked out at all hours of the day to conduct Elite business and search independently for Sabella Gunner, George Griffin, and information about his mother's death.

He was waiting for his friend God to get him the secret book with all The Elite tasks and secrets, but until then, he spent hours each night on the computer searching and talking to his friend and PI Harriet on the phone.

He was exhausted, but I took care of him the best I could and knew he appreciated it, because he told me often.

"Let's go into the stacks," he suggested, his bedroom eyes in full affect. "I want you to get on your knees for me and suck my cock."

I licked my lips subconsciously, imagining how the grain of the carpet would feel on my bare knees as I knelt to undo his pants and take out his beautiful cock.

I'd never known a penis could be beautiful, but Rush's was.

Even though I'd never had experiences with anyone else, I knew because he'd recently introduced me to porn. I'd watch it as he went down on me, then fuck me from behind, just like the couple in the video clip.

I was jerked from my reverie by Rush's phone ringing. I turned back to my work as he spoke quietly into the phone.

"Come on," he said after he hung up, standing to grab my backpack, then pushing all the materials on the desk haphazardly into the open bag. "We've got to go."

"Rush! You've crinkling the pages," I squeaked, ripping the backpack away from him so I could right his mess. "And we shouldn't be going anywhere. I know you're a closeted genius, but some of us need to study for our exams."

Ignoring my protests, he grabbed my hand, interlocking our fingers and tugging me forward. "When God calls, you answer."

I frowned. "I don't think I've ever heard you speak about God in a nice way before."

He laughed, eyes sparkling, cheeks creased like a Hollywood movie star, and there he was, holding *my* hand. "The same could be said for both Gods at one point, but lately, I've warmed up to both. I meant God as in Baxter Goddard V. We're going to his place to plot and hang out with the girlfriends."

I stopped in my tracks. "Seriously?"

"Yeah." He stopped to look back at me and cocked his head to the side. "You don't want to meet them?"

"I'm just…I don't know, nervous," I admitted.

"Because they're all assholes? Don't worry, I'll protect you," he promised with my favorite slow-moving smile.

"No, because they're all your friends. I've never had a boyfriend and I've never had many friends either. What if they don't like me? I'm not cool like them or worldly. Plus, I've seen some of their girls on campus and they're so gorgeous…"

I stopped as Rush stepped closer to gently grasp my chin. "Stop right there. First of all, until you said it, I hadn't really acknowledged my brothers were my friends as well as my fellow crusaders. Probably because I've never been one for having friends myself. Also, there is no way in Heaven or Hell they *won't* like you. All dark things are drawn to the light, and you, my lovely church mouse, shine brighter than anyone I've ever met. Rhett will probably be shamelessly flirting with you in no time just to try to get a rise out of me and Micah will be giving you his number just in case you want a better option than me. Mason and God are difficult motherfuckers, but you'll soothe them just like you soothe me, and they'll love you for it. As for the girls, I don't know them that well, but Zemira will be there, and I think you know her from the orphanage? So you'll have a built-in buddy to show you the way. Now, are we good?"

I blinked at him as I digested the way he'd systematically decimated my worries, then I smiled. "You know, Rush, you're one of the smartest people I know."

He winked at me as he started to lead me forward again. "I know. Just don't tell anyone. It's my best kept secret."

I shouldn't have worried. Not because Rush's brothers weren't intimidating—they totally were—but because aside from briefly ribbing him about me, they largely ignored me so they could have a meeting in another room of God's absurdly huge apartment. That left me with the gorgeous women who'd each claimed a seemingly untameable man.

My palms were sweating and I'd stood there nervously staring at them as they sat around a huge dining room table drinking wine and cocktails like classy urbanites.

"Sit down," Patience, Sam's girlfriend, said with a warm smile. "We aren't going to bite."

"Well, Megan might," Chastity said with a cheeky grin. "But she's into that kinda thing."

"Shut up," Megan told her, but there was humor in her eyes as she did so. "Ignore her, she likes to think I'm the outrageous one, but it's her who always tells people about my sex life."

"Isabelle," Zemira said, standing up to pull me into a hug. "It's good to see you again."

It had been over a year since I'd last check in on her and I felt a pang of guilt for not keeping up with more of the women who aged out of St. Augustine's orphanage, especially girls like her who I'd actually bonded with.

She stepped back, and I noted all the ways she looked different after the accident Rush told me she'd been in. Her beautiful curls were cropped short, but accessorized with a chic gold headband, and she was skinnier than usual, her weight concentrated a little more to one side in favor of a bad leg.

Empathy swelled in my throat, and I pulled her back in for another hug. "I'm sorry for what happened to you," I whispered in her ear. "I wish I could have been there for you."

"I had God," she said strongly, as if the accident was totally behind them both. "But thank you. Now, come sit down and meet the girls."

"The holy virtues," Patience said.

"Patience, we aren't going to call ourselves that," Megan said with a roll of her pretty eyes.

"It's true, though," she protested. "If they're the seven deadly sins, then we're the holy virtues. Their perfect matches."

"Greed doesn't have anyone," Zemira pointed out.

"Doesn't he?" I asked, knowing Rush had been in and out of the house a lot to help Micah with his issues.

Usually, when the boys were in trouble, Rush had told me, a woman was involved.

"Oh my God, seriously!?" Chasity squealed. "I knew he was too good looking to be alone."

We all dissolved into giggles as I finally took a seat and Zemira poured me a glass of wine. We were still laughing, this time over Megan's story about meeting Mason for the first time in a bar, when the boys came back into the room.

Instantly, the air charged with chemistry. I watched with mild fascination as each of the men claimed their women. Mason pulled Megan's hair back by her pony-tail and planted a long, wet kiss on her mouth while Sam picked Patience out of her chair, sat down in it himself, then plunked her back down on his lap. Rhett poked Chastity in her left shoulder, then ducked to her right and kissed her laughing mouth when she finally swiveled the right way, and God carefully, reverently, tipped Z's head back with his fingers on her chin so he could kiss her forehead.

It was so beautiful, it brought tears to my eyes.

Then I felt a tug on my ponytail as Rush pulled the ribbon free and strong, warm hands cupped my neck as he slowly, sensuously slid the ribbon around my throat and retied it there in a bow that was just a little bit too tight.

"How's my church mouse?" he asked me in his long, lazy drawl.

"Accepted, I think," I whispered as I thought about my last hour with the girls. "It feels good."

He pressed a kiss to my unbound hair, then leaned closer to tell me. "God gave me the book."

A thrill shot up my spine. "Should we go home now and read it?"

His chuckle stirred my curls. "No, we have something to talk about with you girls first. You're a part of this too now."

On cue, Rhett cleared his throat and addressed Chastity. "We need to talk about your dad, Chas."

Her face fell immediately into a worried pout. "Do we have to? He's gone now, can't that be enough?"

Rhett looked just as upset about it as she did. "I hate to do anything that could hurt you, you know that, but we have to do something."

"He's hurt a lot of women," Patience said quietly, and Sam took her hand in both of his. "He's hurt me."

"I know he's your dad, Chastity, but he needs to be brought to justice," Mason said in his voice of calm authority.

"I thought The Elite got him out of going to prison?" she asked.

"They did," Rush said slowly. "But that doesn't mean we can't pursue a different kind of justice for him."

"Like what?"

God opened his mouth to speak, but Rhett shot him a subtle, telling look. Chastity did not like God. I didn't know the dynamics of why or how, but it was obvious the guys had spoken about God staying quiet in this discussion.

"He needs help, Chas, and we're going to get it for him," Rhett told her gently. "We're going to put him in a mental institution."

"Where the fucker belongs," Sam said under his breath beside me.

Micah kicked him under the table.

"I guess...I mean, I know that makes sense. He's clearly disturbed and needs help," Chastity admitted. "You promise you won't hurt him, though?"

The men looked at each other, then all nodded curtly with varying degrees of reluctance.

She sighed gustily, then dropped her head back onto Rhett so she should look up at him. "Okay. Do it."

Instantly, the atmosphere in the room relaxed.

"Z said she knows you, Isabelle," God said, clearly happy to be out of the time out corner now that the conversation was over. "From the orphanage?"

"Yeah, I've helped out there since I was young."

He peered at me as he scratched his five o'clock shadow. "How old are you?"

"Twenty-two."

"Older girl," he said, tipping his chin at Rush. "Probably can't keep up with the young ones, hey?"

"Fuck off," Rush said with an easy laugh. "You'd be surprised."

"Don't know it 'til you try it, man," Mason cut in, squeezing Megan's hip. "Older women are fuckin' hot."

I could feel my blush flaming like neon lights from under my skin, but Rush only pulled me back against the chair and combed his fingers through my hair to comfort me. As the conversation raged on around us, rife with good-natured jibes and hearty laughter, Rush leaned down to tell me, "This is how healthy families are together, darlin'. Enjoy it. I know I do."

UINCENDUM NATUS

THIRTEEN

Rush

We were in our robes again, which was not a good sign. First of all, the fabric itched like hell on the back of my neck and it was hot as sin inside the fucking hood given it was late spring in the bayou. Secondly, none of us, not even Pride, who was usually somewhat informed given he was our de facto leader, knew why we had been summoned to the Goddard estate. They'd confiscated our phones a mile back, handed us the goddamn cloaks, and made us hike it the mile left to the mansion.

I smacked a mosquito biting into Rhett like he was a fucking peach.

"The fuck, man?" he asked, pushing me in the shoulder.

"You want to be eaten alive, fine by me," I said with a shrug. "Those things are going at you."

"What can I say? I'm irresistible," Rhett winked at me, and I was reminded, as I often was, why he'd been given the sin of Lust.

"You're such a dipshit," I said, laughing.

"I'm also too hot to die," he groaned dramatically.

Sam caught him in a mock headlock and gave him a noogie. "I'll protect you, princess."

Rhett ducked out of the hold and flipped him off. "Save the caveman shit for Patience."

We all chuckled at their antics, and I knew Rhett had been an ass purposefully to lighten the mood.

It felt good to laugh with my brothers, especially because there was a menace in the dark night that seemed to press in all around us. It was eerie to walk over the fallen magnolia blossom in the wet, black heat toward a future we weren't sure we'd survive. Each and every one of us had reason to think we'd be called to answer for our individual crimes.

I didn't think we were here for something so small. It had to be bigger to warrant so much secrecy and ridiculous ambience.

"This is so stupid," Micah muttered, glaring at the torches as if he could extinguish them with his contempt.

"My dad has never done anything like this, so I don't know what the hell is going on," God admitted quietly, more disturbed than he cared to admit.

Everyone went quiet.

"I guess we're about to find out," I said as we crested the driveway and approached the massive front doors. "If we live, someone come pick my ass up on the way out.

I'm not walking all the way back to our cars. Seriously, fuck that."

My words had their intended effect, and everyone chuckled. The sound was truncated by the sight of eight hooded men waiting to one side of the patio.

One of them stepped forward, the porch lights catching the lower half of his face. I knew before he spoke who it was because of the cruel curl of his smile.

"Good evening, boys," Malcom said, as if welcoming us to some sort of gala or distinguished event. "We have official Elite business to conduct tonight."

"One of our own is to be terminated," Baxter Goddard IV, also known as Four, declared ominously as he waddled forward, looking like a swathed ton of Jell-O in his cloak.

Everyone tensed, no doubt thinking they spoke about Envy.

I knew they weren't. I'd paid to have a man watch the mental hospital where Sebastian was committed and there'd been no movement.

I also knew it wasn't Envy because of something Isabelle had said earlier that day that suddenly made sense.

"I went to my monthly counseling session with Mrs. Griffin today, but she wasn't there," she explained when she arrived home early from classes that afternoon.

I'd paused as I combed through the clerical archives looking for anything to incriminate Archbishop Savoie, a joint in the corner of my mouth. "What?"

"She wasn't there," she said with a shrug as she plucked the joint from my lips to place a kiss there before putting it back.

"Lillian Griffin is always at St. Augustine's," I'd noted

incredulously. "She would literally never miss an opportunity to mess with her students. I looked into it when I joined The Elite. She hasn't had one sick day since she started there, not even when the whole scandal went down with the dean."

Isabelle looked at me for a minute, scouring my face, no doubt noting the shadows under my eyes and the gray cast to my skin from spending too much time at the computer and not enough sleeping. She sighed, then rucked up her dress to climb onto my office chair and straddle my lap. Instantly, her hands went into my hair as she liked to do, threading them through the dense thicket.

"Rush Dempsey, how anyone can call you Sloth is beyond me," she'd murmured, pressing our foreheads together. "You're not only the smartest man I know, but one of the hardest working."

"Not before," I reminded her, rubbing my hands up and down her tiny, hourglass waist. "I have a purpose now to drive me."

"Your mom," she murmured sadly.

"And you. I want to avenge her and protect you."

I blinked away the memory. She'd distracted me from work after that by riding me like she'd been born a cowgirl instead of a church mouse.

I thought about that moment all throughout the fucking feast Four made us sit through before we could actually get down to business. The six of us ate together in a corner away from the rest of The Elite crowding the Goddards' palatial dining hall, but none of us spoke.

Only God and I were unsurprised when Four stepped forward to claim someone among us was a traitor to The Elite and Lillian fucking Griffin was called out for her crimes.

SLOTH

The scene that followed was the most grotesque display of power I'd ever seen in my life. Sam and Mason, the two brothers who had been most wronged by Lillian, pinned her to a chair and systematically overfed her until there was puke coming out of her nose and blood in the vomit spilling from her mouth.

Their fury filled the room like acrid smoke from a fire, singeing my nostrils and layering me in a grimy film of dirt. I felt for my brothers. I'd carried portions of their pain for them when it became too much for them to carry alone. I'd witnessed Sam going through Patience's assault and Sabella's loss, and Mason's bitterness after being unfairly incarcerated for two years and separated from his younger sister.

I *knew* they deserved this vengeance.

Logically, I knew it.

As Sloth, I welcomed it.

But...as Rush Dempsey, as the man who had been reanimated by the honest, faithful heart of good woman, I felt morally and emotionally conflicted watching a human being gorged to death.

Sickness churned in my gut. I let my eyes glaze over with blindness as I continued to stare at the spectacle. I tuned out, thinking of thin, dexterous fingers in my hair, the smell of baby's breath...

"No!" Lillian screeched like a banshee. "You raped me! You made me marry that cheating bastard who loves little teenage whores!"

My mind snapped into the present, and my eyes sharpened on her food-crusted, tear-soaked, bile-splattered face. She continued her diatribe, looking for sympathy from any of the onlookers and finding none.

But her words found me and something clicked.

I tuned out the ordeal, vaguely aware of Four condemning her to death, then suffocating her with his ham-like hand.

I was thinking of her words.

She'd been raped as a girl.

It shouldn't have been significant, but it was.

My brain whirred almost painfully as I tried to bring up the importance of her words. I almost came up blank, but then I remembered a story my mother had once told me when I was a young teenager and she gave me the talk about respecting women.

I was raped as a girl, then, later, when I met your father, I…I felt as if I had to marry him.

It was a stretch to assume Lillian and my mother's pasts had been somehow linked, but something in my gut told me I was onto something.

I looked back at the scene to see Lillian Griffin dead in her chair, sprawled like a used and discarded ragdoll.

"Feed her corpse to the gators, Malcom," Four ordered, as if he was asking a servant to take out the trash. "You owe me for this."

I studied Malcom, who's lips pursed at the command and threat. It was a mistake to underestimate Benedict, even for Four, who owned most of New Orleans and the people in it. Malcom Benedict wasn't a born blue blood. There was something too sly, too willing to be vicious at the slightest provocation or insult.

He stared at Four as he moved over to speak to Sam and Mason. I could read the hate tucked into the corners of his mouth and the creases beside his eyes. That was where I hid mine too.

Sensing my gaze, he looked at me and strolled over when he saw I was separated from my brothers.

"Sloth, you've been a busy bee despite your moniker. I knew I could count on you to take Isabelle Savoie off the board."

I stilled. "It was you who gave me the task, wasn't it?"

When he only smiled mildly at me, a chill ripped down my spine. "You gave me the task because you wanted my father out of the senate so you could take his place. The archbishop and Ward are clearly into something dirty linked to the church and you expect me to exploit it."

Malcom blinked at me. "Well done, boy. Do you want me to give you a prize for your thoughtfulness?"

"You think I'll hand in my own father so you can profit from it?" I asked through gritted teeth, careful to modulate my voice so none of the acolytes clearing the door and the dead body of Lillian Griffin could overhear us.

"I think you'll do anything to avenge your dear old mom's death," he amended. "God should have the book by now, has he given it to you?"

My gaze whipped to my friend, who was speaking passionately to his father.

How did Malcom know God had handed it over to me? My instinct was to blame God, to storm over and demand what kind of game he was playing, but Isabelle had taught me to believe in the goodness of people and I knew God wouldn't throw us to the proverbial wolves by telling Malcom our secrets. No, Malcom had to have guessed we'd been his good little minions and done exactly what he wanted. I wondered what would happen if I proved him wrong. So I lied.

"He will," I said mildly, sliding my hands into my pockets as if I didn't have a single care in the fucking world.

Malcom smiled at me. "I have to give credit where credit is due, you have balls of steel. A man like you, logical, unattached...I could use you."

"I'd rather set myself on fire," I countered pleasantly. "But thanks for the compliment."

"I'll be seeing you soon," he said as I moved away from him. "When you bring me the book."

I tossed a mock salute to him over my shoulder and went to join the rest of my group, but a chill of foreboding fused my spine together too tight, and I walked with the pain of it for the rest of the night.

Hours later, when dawn was casting gray shadows over New Orleans like the fingers of a fucking specter, I opened the door to my house and found Isabelle curled up on the couch in the foyer. She had clearly waited up for me and fell asleep. Something twanged in my heart, then smoothed out as I walked over to stare down at her peaceful face and wild mass of curls. I pushed the locks away from her face and crouched down beside her to place a kiss on her sleep soft lips.

It was selfish of me, but I needed to lose myself in her to forget the very real horrors of tonight.

She stirred slightly, thick lashes fluttering and lips pursing.

I kissed her again, then spoke against her cheek. "Wake up, darlin'. I need you to help me chase away my demons."

Her eyes opened, light brown like amber in the low light. Instantly, her hand raised to my cheek and pressed there to comfort me.

I didn't deserve that kind of wholesome attention, but fuck me if I wasn't going to take it anyway.

"What happened?" she asked in her sweetly accented French voice. "You're so cold."

I swallowed thickly, trying to give voice to the filth I felt coating every inch of my skin. "The Elite executed Lillian Griffin tonight."

I wanted to tell her Sam and Mason had done most of the work with their bare hands, but I wanted to protect my brothers from Isabelle's censure. She'd heard the stories, but she hadn't *lived* them. She couldn't understand how the need for vengeance was branded on our souls and flared to life like Harry Potter's lightning bolt scar whenever we had the opportunity to enact it.

She sat up abruptly, spinning her legs over the end of the couch to bracket my body as her hands went up to cup my face. I was momentarily distracted by the silk of her little nighty catching at her nipples and over her hips. Slowly, over the last few weeks, I'd been buying her new clothes to replace the spinster rags she'd worn before. Last weekend, we'd even gone shopping and she gave me a fashion show in Victoria's Secret.

"Rush, focus," she said, pulling my gaze up from her tits to her face. "They *killed* someone tonight? Are you okay?"

I let out a gusty exhale. "I can't decide if I want to get high as Benny Franklin's kite or go to fucking confessional."

She studied my face, her thumbs sweeping soothingly over my cheeks. "Why don't we do both?"

I blinked at her in shock, which made her laugh.

"I know, I know, I don't normally push you to smoke,

but I think this is a special circumstance. You grab what you need, and I'll get changed and meet you back here. Call Buford. We're going to church.'"

"I don't think it's a good idea to go back to the cathedral. Your father has left us alone by some small miracle, but we shouldn't push our luck."

She snorted and rolled her eyes. I loved that every day we were together she was cultivating her own brand of sass and gumption. "Please, my father is leaving us alone because he knows I wouldn't last one day with you without becoming spoiled goods. I'm of no use to him now. Anyway, I wasn't thinking of that church."

Half an hour later, the Rolls pulled up to the same cracked pavement parking lot I'd been to numerous times since joining The Elite.

It was the site of the abandoned nunnery.

A chill rushed down my spine as I stared at the crumbling structure at the crest of the hill, the sky over it a portentous plume of dark gray clouds. I took Isabelle's hand tightly in my own as we ascended the gentle slope, the disintegrating headstones in the cemetery like religious trash strewn about the nunnery's front yard.

"You come here to pray?" I asked her warily.

This did not seem like a place of worship. It was a place The Elite conducted their business, where Pride doled out the despicable tasks to overeager sinners.

"I know it seems kind of creepy, but it's private. Whenever I wanted to truly talk to God without my father interfering, I always came here," she explained as we reached the molding wooden door and she pushed inside.

It smelled of mildew and toxic earth, cobwebs so old, they seemed calcified in the corners of the room.

I'd checked my cameras for any signs of strange Elite activities, but the only people who came and went from the nunnery were my brothers and me.

Still, I was convinced this was a place of evil. I shuddered as Isabelle led from the small main room into the chapel at the back. It was somehow colder than the air outside, but the temperature had better preserved the few rows of pews and the old stone altar where a plain wooden crucifix hung.

We knelt before the altar, still holding hands even though Isabelle bent her head in prayer. I studied her for a few moments before I asked, "What the hell am I supposed to do?"

A breath of laughter escaped her. "Try not to be blasphemous in Chapel, Rush. You can do whatever you want. When I speak to God, it's a private conversation and very individualistic. You can ask Him questions, tell Him your story, or just meditate on what happened tonight and see where He leads your thoughts."

Kneeling hurt my knees, and the mildew scent tickled my nose so hard, it made me want to sneeze, but I stayed there on the ground. Not just for Isabelle, because I knew it meant something to her for me to discover my more spiritual side, but also because I'd been desperate for guidance, for hope and faith, for a very long time.

It wouldn't hurt to try this God character out, though, in my personal opinion, I thought if any gender was going to be a holy entity, it would be female. Every man I knew was a sinner of the first fucking order.

I closed my eyes, bent my head like Isabelle, and waited for His light or whatever to show me the way.

Nothing happened.

Five minutes passed into ten. The sun winked over the horizon, signaling a new day, but no new thoughts came to me. I focused on Lillian, on how much she deserved to die and how much I wanted to enact the same kind of justice on my father, Malcom, and Envy—any fucker with a hand in The Elite's fucked dealings.

Only, my brothers and I were The Elite. Did that mean I would condone us all to Hell along with the rest of them?

When I signed up, I'd known my goal was to end the society, but some of them, like Rhett, had actually wanted to join for the power and success they could reap from it.

Did I absolve them of their sins because they weren't as grave as the laundry list of depravities committed by the others?

It probably wasn't moral, but the answer came easily to me.

Fuck yes, I'd fucking absolve them.

We were basically still kids with our futures before us. We needed to be opportunistic and self-centered to a certain extent to figure out the best way to live out our lives. After every atrocity they'd committed on behalf of the society, my brothers had seen the darkness of The Elite and vowed to end them.

It wasn't the religious moment of enlightenment typical of stories in the bible or other religious texts, but it was enough for us. We were sinners, after all. Nothing was going to change that.

When I grew bored of thinking in the vacuum of my own mind, I peered at Isabelle, who's sweet pink mouth was moving softly as she spoke to her God. I was reminded, looking at my woman in her virginal white dress kneeling on an altar like a maiden sacrifice, the closest I'd ever felt to God was between her legs.

Quietly, so I would interrupt her, I walked on my knees to just behind her, then laid on the floor propped up by my elbows so I could get the right angle. I pushed at the small of her back so her spine curved and her ass popped out perfectly me for to cup and tilt with my hands.

"Rush," she gasped as she braced herself on the floor. "What are you doing?"

"Praying," I told her as I pulled down her panties just enough to reveal her pretty pussy. "The only way I know how."

Before she could say another word, I lifted my head to close my mouth over her pussy, opening her cleft with my hands so I could delve my tongue deep inside her.

She shivered and moaned softly, but she didn't move.

My church mouse knew I needed her sweetness against my tongue, her scent in my nose, and her body near mine in order to feel right again. She was my purification, my absolution, and the only fucking deity I needed to feel whole.

I wrapped one of my hands over her thigh so I could lift up her skirt in the front and play with her hard clit as I raked my tongue in her dampening folds, from her entrance to her puckered asshole.

She gasped. "Oh my God, Rush."

A perverse triumph swept through me hearing her take the God's name in vain because of me, because I brought her closer to Heaven. I ate at her until her juices covered my chin like spilled holy water and her thighs quaked around my ears.

"I'm going to come," she whispered, and a moment later, she broke apart on my tongue.

I licked up her juices, feeling both wicked and liberated by her release.

"Brace yourself on the altar," I told her roughly as I gripped her hip with her skirt scrunched up in one fist and opened my fly to pull out my aching cock. "I'm going to give you every throbbing inch of my cock and you're going to take it all, aren't you, Isabelle?"

She shivered at my words, but didn't responded. She was still too aware we were in a holy place. I was possessed with the need to splinter her resolve and make her realize the truth of this thing between us.

That we were the holiest thing in the place.

"Tell me how much you want my thick dick inside you," I ordered as I rubbed the head of my hot cock against her dripping opening.

Her hips bucked back against me and she panted hard, but still no words.

I wrapped her ribbon tied hair in one of my fists, the other in a tight vice around one of her sweet ass cheeks as I slid an inch in and out of her heat. "Tell me what I want to hear, Church Mouse. Tell me you want me more than anything else, that you love me more than anything—even your God."

"Fuck," she burst out as she jerked her hips back and impaled herself on my cock. "Fuck me, Rush. I love you, I love you, I love you."

"More than anything?" I growled as I used her hair like reins to pull her on and off my erection in a painfully slow rhythm. "I'll fuck you just how you like if you tell me what I want to hear."

"Yes," she whimpered, grinding back onto me in desperation. "Yes, I love you more than anything, even Him. Now please, Rush, love me too."

So I did. I fucked her hard from behind until she came all over my cock, washing me in her juices like a sexual baptism. It gave me the idea I needed to bring on a soul crushing orgasm.

"On your knees for me," I barked out as I stood on shaking legs, jerking my angry red cock so forcefully, it was almost painful.

She spun around on her knees for me, flushed and used like a dirtied angel on the altar of the chapel.

"Open your mouth and take my cum."

As she parted her red lips, the orgasm hit me like a fucking runaway freight train.

A long groan ripped from the fabric of my throat as I pumped my cock and my cum rained down all over Isabelle's beautiful, angelic face, painting her in my essence, claiming her as my very own.

I stared down at her as I squeezed the last drop from my dick and watched it land on her outstretched tongue, feeling more powerful and at peace than I ever had before.

"Delicious," Isabelle said with a little giggle as she licked her lips. "But very messy."

I chuckled as I did up my pants before dropping to my knees and pulling my mother's old handkerchief from my wallet to wipe off Isabelle's face. Her hand grabbed my wrist when I was done and held it to my cheek so she could kiss my still thundering pulse.

"I do love you, you know, more than anything else," she said softly, her huge eyes wide with sincerity and endless tenderness.

My heart throbbed like a fucking open wound in my chest as I stared at the loving expression on her beloved face. I swallowed thickly before I could croak, "Fuck me, I love you too. So fucking much it hurts."

She placed a soothing hand on my chest, then a calming kiss to my lips, gentling me like a cowgirl with a restless stallion in a way only she could.

"Let's go home. It's been a long night for you. Even though I don't think you got quite what I wanted you to out of this experience, I still think it was healing."

I laughed as I stood up and helped her to her feet. "Definitely healing. You fixed me with your holy pussy."

"Rush," she squealed, pushing me into the confessional as we passed it. "You're impossible."

I grinned as I pushed off against the paneling, then frowned as it gave way beneath my hand with a soft creak.

"The fuck..." I muttered as the door to the confessional opened and cold, dank air swirled out.

I stepped inside the amazingly conserved wooden confessional and notice the draft came from a gap under the back wall of the box. My heart kicked into a canter as I pressed my hands to the wood and pushed into it at different sections, hoping and wondering wildly if it would open a secret latch.

"It's just an old door, Rush. I don't think..." Isabelle trailed off when my fingers found a small button built into the edge of the wood and the back panel pushed open with a creepy groan.

I stepped through the secret door and waited for my eyes to adjust to the gloomy interior.

We were in a small room with a single high, barred window cut into the far wall and a rusty bed frame without a mattress tucked into one corner. The floor was packed earth, stained in places from liquids I could only guess at identifying.

"What is this place?" Isabelle asked as she moved into the room behind me, hugging her arms around herself to stave off the chill.

I walked toward the bed and peered beneath it to see if there was any clue to what this place could have been used for, but there was nothing to be found. As I continued to search every corner, Isabelle went over to the frame and sat down tentatively on the rusted springs.

I turned around to tell her to be careful, but lost my train of thought when she reached out to the wall to trace her finger over something.

"The woman you killed tonight..." she breathed, "it was Lillian?"

I nodded.

"Her name is carved into the stone," she said in horror.

"It could be anyone," I rationalized before I got too excited about the discovery. "It isn't an unusual name."

"No," she whispered, tracing her finger over another mark even lower down. "But the name Magnolia is."

I froze, then started to run across the room to see the inscription for myself when my boot caught against something jutting from the earthen ground.

"Rush!" Isabelle cried out as I fell. "Are you okay?"

"Yeah," I said, but my voice sounded distant to my own ears as I rolled to a seated position to check out what I'd tripped over. "I just fell over something."

I used my fingers to brush off the dirt and unearth the round protrusion that had tripped me up. It was lodged so deeply in the ground, I had to use my fingers and nails like claws, then leverage my entire weight against it to break it free.

Something splintered at the base and fell back as I came away with part of it in my hand.

"Oh my God," Isabelle screamed as she saw what I held aloft before I could right myself and look at it properly.

I stared in horror at the human bone cradled in my palm.

"Holy fuck," I rasped.

"We have to call the police," Isabelle said as she clamored off the bed to the ground beside me and tossed the bone from my numb hand. "This is way beyond us, Rush. This is pure evil."

I heard her speaking, but the words didn't register. My mind was working through a problem.

"Do you have the book in your purse still?" I asked her in hollow voice. I'd given it to her for safe keeping. No one was likely to think the church mouse was carrying a metaphorical bomb in her bag.

"Rush, I think you're in shock. We need to call the police and—"

"Do. You. Have. The. Book?" I gritted out between my clenched teeth.

Acid was starting to burn holes in my body as a revelation began to surge to the surface of my brain. Isabelle sensed my urgency and rushed out of the room to grab her purse where she'd dropped it at the opening to the confessional.

When she returned, I took it from her hands and noticed my fingers were shaking.

"Go back over to the wall and tell me if you see any of the names I say, okay?" I asked her as I flipped through the sin-soaked pages of the book to the part I remembered with the women's names and series of letters beside them.

She did as I said quietly and quickly.

"L.B.," I whispered. "Lillian Benedict."

"Yes."

"Hannah Kempt or H.K."

"Yes," Isabelle confirmed in a shaky voice again and again as I listed names and she found them crudely etched into the wall near the bed.

Finally, my eyes landed on the initials I'd been dreading. "M.LB. Magnolia LeBlanc."

"Yes, Rush," she whispered through her tears. "She's here."

"Fuck," I said, dropping the book and resting my forehead on my raised knees as I fought furious tears. "What the fuck is this place?"

"I recognize some of the names," Isabelle said as she crawled over the floor to me and wrapped me in her arms. "We need to confirm with Zemira, but I think they're the names of the girls who ran away from St. Augustine's orphanage."

My throat burned as I swallowed the information and digested the horrific conclusion. "They didn't run away, The Elite brought them here."

VII

UINCENDUM NATUS

FOURTEEN

Isabelle

I left Rush asleep in bed.

He wanted to call his brothers right away and tell them what we'd found, but I convinced him that even though we made a break through, we still didn't have enough to incriminate anyone for crimes and it could wait until later that day after he finally got some rest. He'd been convinced he wouldn't sleep, but after a few moments in my arms in bed, he was out like an exhausted little boy, his face troubled even in sleep.

He wouldn't wake up for hours, and I only needed one to get there, do what I needed to do, and get back before he noticed I was gone.

The only problem was I hadn't driven a car in a long time and I wasn't about to call Buford to drive me because he'd wake up Rush to get the go-ahead. So, I opened the door to the free-standing garage beside Rush's house and flipped on the light. Illuminated in the soft yellow light were my boyfriend's "pleasure" vehicles for when he actually felt like driving himself.

A red Tesla roadster, a black Range Rover sport, and a green Lamborghini.

I stared at the cars for a minute, then the keys hanging neatly by the door before I grabbed the set for the Lambo.

I figured if I was going to be bad, I might as well go all out.

The engine came to life with a throaty purr and I couldn't help but stroke the luxurious wheel in my hands a few times before I pulled out of the garage into the midday sun. I struggled to adjust to the stick shift and the easy glide of the car over the asphalt, but the new experience thrilled me. It wasn't a long ride to St. Augustine's, but driving such a gorgeous car made the task I had to accomplish a lot more palatable.

It was a Tuesday, early afternoon, so there wouldn't be any events happening in the cathedral, but tourists also added it to their itineraries and it was one of the most popular times of the year for them to visit, so I wasn't surprised when I pulled up to see people milling in and out.

I held my breath as I walked up the steps through the front doors, my heart fighting to break the cage of my ribs with each beat.

I didn't know what would happen if my father saw me, dressed in a nice, form fitting dress tied with a bow at the collar, red gloss on my lips and mascara on my eyelashes. He would call me a harlot, no doubt. Delilah reincarnate. If he could get away with it, he might pinch me, slap me, or kick me.

I hoped he was busy entertaining the tourists or working enclosed in his office, not to be disturbed.

There were a handful of people walking around the marble space as I entered, but I kept an eye out as I rounded the right side of the pews and walked down the hall to my tiny office and the adjoining library I shared with various church volunteers.

One of those volunteers had been Magnolia.

I let out a deep breath when I closed the library door behind me and quickly set to searching through the separate cubicles that held each person's work notes and paraphernalia. It was a disorganized mess I'd been meaning to get to, but at the moment, I was glad I hadn't. It meant that no one had cleaned out Magnolia's station.

A sneeze ripped through me, echoing in the empty room, and I was quick to cover the next one with my sleeve before I unearthed more dusty files.

After ten tense minutes of searching, I found what I was looking for.

A leather portfolio like they used in the eighties and nineties embossed in gold on the front with the name Magnolia Ward. I fell from my knees onto my bottom and unzipped the contents.

Sheaves of papers spilled over my lap and onto the floor, most of them filled margin to margin in cramped, slanted handwriting. I could feel the thrum of my heart like a hummingbird in my chest as I picked them up one by one until something caught my attention.

Hannah Kempt.

Kelsey Westcott.

Bridget Haines.

Lisa McGivern…

The list of names went on and on, three columns across and filled from top to bottom on each side of the page. There were small Roman numerals every few names that I deciphered quickly to mean the date.

Lillian Benedict was there, not too long after Magnolia LeBlanc.

I bit my fist to keep the scream inside my chest as I read the notes of the next page and realized Magnolia had kept some kind of record complete with a legend of the women from the orphanage who had gone missing, their ages, and their date of departure.

There were a series of initials beside each name too, sometimes one and sometimes more. It reminded me of the initials we had seen in The Elite book God had given Rush. Somehow, they were linked.

Voices approached outside the hall, and I quickly stuffed everything I could back into the portfolio before zipping it shut. I tucked it under my arm, took a deep breath, and exited the library as if I'd never stopped working there.

"Isabelle?" a voice immediately asked just as I closed the door behind me. "Isabelle? It is you? I haven't seen you in weeks."

I turned with a wooden smile to face Mr. Jefferson, a kind elderly man who was one of my father's most dedicated flock.

"Hello, Mr. Jefferson. It's lovely to see you. I've been… out of town visiting my mother's family in France and learning about the religious practices there. It's been very enlightening," I lied through my teeth, surprised by the easiness of the deception passing through my lips and the fact that God didn't immediately strike me down for being dishonest in his home.

"Always a good girl, you were." He grinned a gap-toothed smile at me. "In fact, I was just telling your father how much we missed your sunny smile around here."

I tried not to bolt in a panic. "Is he around today?"

Mr. Jefferson frowned. "Are you not working here any-more? He told me you were."

"Yes, of course...um, if you'll just excuse me, I have class to get to," I told him rudely as I backed away. "Give Mrs. Jefferson my regards."

I spun around and hurried down the hall, dashing around the corner blindly in my desperation to get out of the hell I'd once thought was home.

Two hands clamped like steel fixtures to my shoulders and I looked wide eyed and breathless into my father's irate face.

"Isabelle," he murmured so no one else would hear the menace in his tone. "So good of you to finally come home."

"I'm not," I said, but my voice broke and gave away my anxiety. "I have a new home and a new life."

"Don't be ridiculous. Your place is here with your father and your God."

His fingers tightened painfully around my biceps.

"No, my place is with Rush, and *my* God is a different being than yours. He doesn't believe in black and white, and He wants me to be happy so long as it does no harm to others."

"You don't have any authority on the matter," he started to preach, but I cut him off.

"You don't have any either. The Elite gave you this job when your football career didn't work out and instead of embracing God and His light, you just used it as a means of power for yourself. They could take it all away from you tomorrow and..." my face twisted into a sneer with hatred, "you. Would. Be. *Fucked.*"

His face glowed red with anger, a vein popping in his temple. "Don't you dare talk to me like that. I raised you to be better than this."

"You didn't raise me, you *groomed* me. And I'll talk to you the way you deserve," I retorted, feeling his rage contaminate me. "You are the worst kind of bully and a horrible father. Truly, I hope I never see you again."

I wanted to rail at him for the abuse and for what I now suspected he'd done in helping The Elite abduct young orphans, but I wanted to get out of there unscathed and back to Rush more.

"Listen to me—" my father began to demand again.

"Never again," I vowed, wrenching myself painfully out of his hold, then rushing toward the doors.

I flung them open, the portfolio in one hand, and ran down the steps to the Lambo, not once looking back even though I could feel his eyes tracking me like a predator. I started the car and squealed out of the lot, only really breathing when I was blocks away and the fact that I'd survived my first confrontation with my father began to settle in.

Then, I smiled.

Rush

My footsteps echoed through the empty house, clipped and evenly spaced like the tick of a clock counting down to an explosion. I had my hands in my pockets, but they were clenched tight into fists, my anger concentrated in each curled digit so it wouldn't spill into my countenance and ruin the surprise.

I rounded the corner and stepped into my father's open office.

He was seated, as he usually was, behind his enormous antique desk with every item aligned meticulously on the surface and his three phones arranged in a row beside his right hand. He worked from home most of the time, delegating to the masses of people who did most of the heavy lifting for him.

He didn't seem surprised to see me, but then, I'd never seen him surprised by anything.

Not even my mother's death.

"Hey, Daddy-o," I greeted with a mock salute before jamming my hand back into my pocket and strolling over to the seat across from him to perch on the arm. "How goes it?"

"What do you want, Rush? If you've come to apologize, it's too late. You willingly participated in killing Lillian and you know she was an asset to this family."

"Did I?" I shrugged, because honestly, she seemed like a fucking disloyal wild card to me. "I think I'm confused. Who comes first, The Elite or the Dempseys?"

"Me," he said immediately, with all his considerable authority. "I come first, for you and for this family."

It was no surprise he'd been named Pride back in his initiation phase.

Rage burned low in my throat, turning my voice to smoke and ash. "So, when Mom told you she couldn't live with keeping your secrets for you anymore, you threatened her the same way you threatened me last time I was here?"

Ward was always still, but he turned to granite at my words, not a breath of air escaping him.

"I ask because it seems obvious if you threatened her life when she wanted to expose you for organizing an underage sex ring through St. Augustine's Cathedral and orphanage. Hell, I only threatened to take you down for Mom's murder, and I didn't even have any evidence when he did it. Mom had more than evidence, she *lived* it, didn't she? She was one of the first girls taken from the orphanage and kept in that hellacious nunnery. Did you kill the ones no one took a fancy to? We found bones in the ground there. I guess, in a way, Mom was lucky you liked her enough to marry her in the first place."

"That's not how it works," Ward cut in, his voice singed at the edges with wrath. "Yes, girls died, but it was never because we wanted to get rid of them. Sometimes, with their preferences, the men got too rough and it was inevitable a few would get lost along the way."

"You're disgusting," I said with all the abhorrence I felt at sharing the same fucking blood as him. "You're a fucking abomination."

"I'm a fucking success," he told me. "I'm one of the most influential leaders in the United States government because I know what needs to be done to get to the top, to win. I won't apologize for doing what I had to do as a young man to get to where I am today."

"Even though it cost innocent young women their lives?"

"They weren't so innocent. You think Lillian Benedict just ended up there? Her brother, Malcom, didn't have to complete a task to get into The Elite. His family *is* The Elite. Still, he sold out his sister to George Griffin to strength his allegiances in the society and show that he was committed to our cause. Magnolia? Her own father *sold* her to the last archbishop to get himself out of a bind with the mafia. They just exchanged one evil for another. Those girls were never going to be free."

"So, you used them."

It was so easy to him, like math or physics, the girls just numbers making up an equation on the page that equaled his success.

I felt sick just being in the same room with the motherfucker.

"You think you're so smart for figuring this out, but you have no proof. The Elite keeps their records safe and well-hidden," he told me smugly.

I checked my Rolex Daytona for the time, then looked up at him with an easy shrug. "Maybe…if you hadn't made enemies within The Elite. But you did, and now I have the book and Mom's records of the kidnapped girls. It took me a second to figure out the initials beside each girl's name, but when I did, it was fucking obvious. W.D. for Magnolia, M.B. for Lillian, and a dozen G.Gs. Ward Dempsey, Malcom Benedict, and George Griffin."

"You think that means something, don't you? Well, you are proving yourself ignorant and pathetic as always, Rush. The Elite own the New Orleans police, one of our members owns New Orleans News and Media; who do you think will arrest and defame us?"

I sighed and my shoulder's slumped in defeat. "You're right, what was I thinking?"

"You weren't," Ward said smugly. "You never do."

I looked up at him with my head tipped down. "You always underestimated me, dad. I was just the lazy, wicked son without proper ambition. The second your actions spurred mom to kill herself you lit a fire under that 'lazy' ass and I got motivated real quick.

"Do you remember your task from The Elite? If I recall correctly, as Pride you had to publicly humiliate St. Augustine's football hero. You probably aren't aware that four years later, the man dubbed Lust raped his sister in the pursuit of his task. The Elite ruined that family just as they've ruined so many others…It's just my luck that Liam Jaccard is now Director of Criminal Investigations and his sister, Taylor, works at CNN."

I watched the sunset in my father's eyes and his face grow dark with furious indignation.

"We have the papers, the nunnery filled with fucking bones in a secret fucking sex room, and we have this conversation," I said, pulling my recording phone from my pocket. "Seriously, Daddy Dearest, I never thought you'd be too lazy to talk to me about this without checking to see if I was recording it on my fucking phone."

"I'll end you," my father said.

"Too late," I told him as a loud commotion exploded at the front door and police officers and the FBI began to file in down the hall. "I've already ended you."

VII

UINCENDUM NATUS

FIFTEEN

arriet found George in Iowa shacked up with an underage farmer's daughter, which didn't surprise any of us. I sent Buford there with her to transport him back on God's private plane. My brothers and I met them at a landing strip in the bayou, a private airspace owned by Goddard Oil and Gas.

We didn't want anyone asking any questions about why a screaming man, cuffed and bruised, was being hustled off a plane without his consent.

I also knew what would happen the moment Sam saw George Griffin's foot land on the tarmac.

He launched himself forward, moving with surprising speed for such a massive guy, even Micah and Mason couldn't reach out to grab him in time.

I could have told them to be prepared to hold him back, but I didn't.

SLOTH

The ex-dean didn't deserve even the smallest of mercies.

Buford made eye contact with me from where he stood holding the man fifteen yards away, waiting for my signal. Subtly, I nodded, and Buford stepped behind George, yanking his arms back so he was held immobile.

Sam's fist descended like Thor's hammer on George's jaw with a resounding *crack* that carried across the asphalt.

Blood spilled from his mouth over his white shirt, carrying a few teeth with it to the ground.

Sam landed another meaty blow to his temple, and George's legs gave out from under him. Happily, Buford was there to hold him up.

I looked over at my brothers, who stood glaring, but immobile. We all knew Sam was in a dangerous place. One wrong move, one more mistake, and his mind would dissolve into darkness just as surely as Envy's had.

Mason raised an eyebrow at me, more than aware I had planned for this just like I planned for everything.

I grinned sharply at him then strolled over to Sam and George.

"Stop," I told Sam when I was a foot behind him.

"Are you fucking kidding me? The bastard deserves it," Sam growled, turning on me with a snarl, his huge hands fisted.

"Dude, we agreed not to kill Chas's father," Rhett said as he came up behind me. "Lay the fuck off before you do something we'll all regret."

"You're the only one who will regret it," Sam snapped. "Just because your precious girlfriend can't part with her fucked up daddy."

"Watch yourself," Rhett barked, stepping forward threateningly.

God appeared next to him, clamping a strong hand over his shoulder. "Brother, stand down."

"We did," I mused, pulling at my lower lip as if I was just now formulating a plan. "But we never said we wouldn't hurt him."

"Rush," Rhett rumbled.

"Chastity will never know," Mason pointed out. "None of us will tell her."

"You're saying you won't tell your girl and she won't tell mine?" Rhett argued rationally.

Our girls were all tight, almost as tight as we were.

But not quite.

"Yeah, brother," Mason vowed quietly, soberly. "We won't tell anyone."

Rhett looked us each in the eye, reading our agreement written in our own blood like an irrevocable oath. He sighed and scratched the back of his head. "Fuck, fine. God knows the fucker deserves it."

Sam grinned menacingly, then reared back to deliver another punch to the gagged ex-dean.

I caught his fist and waited for him to look back at me before I reached into my pocket and placed something in his hand.

"We need a reason to admit George to the asylum. Showing up with him beaten to shit and our knuckles busted up isn't going to inspire them to take him in," I pointed out.

"I'll pay them off," God said, as if I was a moron. "Anyone can be bought."

"True. But if we make it look like he practices self-harm to the point of suicide, they'll put him on a concoction of drugs that will leave him just as broken and vegetal as Envy. Lifelong payback," I explained.

Sam wrenched his hand out of my grip and stared at the whip I'd put between his fingers. "I'm guessing this is part of that plan?"

"In Christianity there's a practice called self-flagellation. A man with impure thoughts will flog himself to purge his body of sin and wrongdoings," I said, looking down into George Griffin's eyes as they bulged with fear. "I think little old George here is in need of some serious purification."

Sam's eyes lit on fire as he tested the weight of the whip in one hand. "Who wants to hold him down?"

A gurgled whimper came from George and we all turned to watch him pee his pants.

"I'm not carry that lump of shit," God called, staring at him in revulsion.

Micah stepped forward to help Buford drag him into the small, empty cargo holding room beside the tarmac. We watched as he collected a few zip-ties from the collection of supplies by the door, then cuffed him to a pulley hanging from the ceiling. The sound of rending fabric ripped through the room as he used a switch blade to slice George's shirt down the back so it fell open to reveal his white spine.

Sam moved immediately. "Hold him tight."

Mason took up his other side, and together ,with Micah, they held him down while Sam began to beat him.

The sharp slap of the whip connecting and splitting skin cracked through the air.

We watched mesmerized as yet another one of our enemies fell at our feet, pathetic and fucking destroyed.

The sounds grew wet, the drips of blood to the floor and the sucking smack of the whip against his back as Sam systematically tore at his flesh.

He stopped, panting, arm shaking.

God sighed dramatically, taking the bloody whip from him. "Chastity hates me anyway, why don't you let me finish him off?"

Sam stared at him with a tight jaw, so consumed with fury, it didn't seem like he could physically stop himself.

God clasped him by one shoulder and pressed his forehead to Sam's sweat drenched one. "Let me help you, brother. Let me give the fucker what he deserves. My retribution is your retribution."

Sam squeezed his eyes shut as sweat dripped into his eyes, then swiped at it with one bloody hand, smearing red across his face like battle paint.

"Make it hurt," he ordered as he stepped back.

God looked over his shoulder at Rhett who stood with his arms crossed and his brow creased as if he hated what we were doing.

But there was a savage light in his eyes that said he enjoyed the righteous violence as much as we did.

He nodded slightly.

Then George Griffin was purged of his guilt with the whip once more, until he was an empty lump of flesh bleeding his sins across the floor.

"You're a charmer, aren't you?"

The pretty nurse, Nori, who spoke to me last time I

visited Envy in Baton Rouge smiled down at Sebastian as he sat eating in the cafeteria.

It was cruel, but Rhett had paid her to flirt with him a little, get him riled up and excited so the fall would be even more devastating when we ripped him away from the safety of the hospital and threw him into the flames of our fury. George was already resting in a room down the corridor, drugged up the way he would be for the rest of his life. It had been even easier than we thought to get him admitted. Rhett had told the receptionist the circumstances of George's mental break with one of his winning smiles, God had greased the palm of the hospital administrator and viola! George Griffin was officially Sebastian Westbrook. If anyone went looking for George, they wouldn't find him, and if anyone checked in on Sebastian, they'd find him still rotting away in the hospital.

One justice was served and we were ready for the next.

Sebastian grinned, the shape wonky because of the cocktail of drugs fucking up his system. "Oh, you have no idea."

"Oh," she countered softly, "I think I do."

I looked down at my phone as it buzzed with an incoming text.

Harriet: I got something. Call me.

Me: I'm busy with the last thing you got for me.

Harriet: Make time for this. I found the key to unlock The Elite completely.

I looked down at the message for a long minute, daring to hope Harriet had found the last nail to put in the coffin of The Elite.

Micah tensed beside me, drawing my focus to his

face, which was set in stone as he stared at my phone in my hand.

"Who is Harriet?" he demanded quietly.

"Why do you care?" I countered, staring at him closely enough to see the veins throb in his forearms as he clenched his fists, his eyes ablaze with protective anger.

He jerked his chin up in silent demand for me to go first.

"She's my P.I., and before you go off, I trust her completely. She found George and she's looking for Sabella."

Micah practically calcified beside me, his jaw so clenched he had to be damaging his teeth.

"You know something," I breathed as my heart rate kicked up.

A muscle jumped in his cheek.

"Tell me. If you can't trust me, who can you trust?"

"No one with this," he ground out, then shifted slightly toward me when Mason looked over at us. "But if it will shut you up, we'll talk later."

I stared at him hard, then nodded. "Only trying to help, man."

"Should'a known you'd nose in," Micah muttered as he looked back over at Sebastian and Nori. "Always showing up when we don't fucking want you too."

I grinned. "And look at how many times I've saved your asses."

"I was the one who saved someone this time," he retorted. "Now, shut the fuck up."

I swallowed my excitement and my irritation at him keeping something potentially important from his brothers and tried to focus on our current mission.

Sebastian was watching Nori, licking his lips like a

feral wolf as she walked away toward where we all waited in the hallway.

We made eye contact and I winked at her just to see a real blush and giddy smile spread across her face.

"Sebastian!" she turned to call to him.

He jumped in his seat, then stood slightly, ready to run to her, already thinking about what sick things he would do to her if he could just get her alone.

"Your brothers are here for you."

He froze, his ass hovering over his seat. "What?"

"You heard me," she said as she folded her arms, her voice gone cold.

"Which one?" he asked, fear thick in his voice.

"All of them," I said, stepping forward into the room, my brothers at my back. "We've come to take you home."

VII

UINCENDUM NATUS

SIXTEEN

Rush

One week later.

They appeared out of the midnight dark one by one, the faint light from the full moon gilding their black hoods in silver as they took their place in a half circle before me.

Normally, it was Pride at their center, but tonight, it was me.

Mason had been our leader when Lillian was in charge, but she was gone.

God had stepped in after that when his father, Four, still owned New Orleans and Goddard Oil and Gas, but now, he too was dead.

So, with those two, my father, and the archbishop of New Orleans in jail, it was my turn to put the final nail in the coffin of The Elite.

It was a final act I'd been working toward since the moment I'd joined the society. Only...I'd never known it was going to end like this.

Ironically, it was going to end with the final completion of my task.

Desecrating St. Augustine's Cathedral.

"We joined The Elite knowing it was for life. We agreed to be given an action to perform to show our dedication to the society and our willingness to let it shape us and our futures. We agreed to it, but at the time, we didn't truly understand it. Now, after everything that has happened to us, we know the depravity within the society and the darkness within ourselves. The difference between the two factions is that unlike The Elite, we have made the decision to accept our virtues as well as our sins."

I took a deep breath, unused to speeches or the spotlight. I was the kind of man who liked to operate in the shadows, behind the screen of computers and hands of many other people doing my work in my stead. It was an out of body experience to lead my brothers, but it was one I needed to experience and one they needed me to explore.

After all, only I could have set up the elements of tonight's final Elite ceremony.

"When we killed Lillian, I asked myself what set us apart from the rest of those miserable fuckers—and it was exactly that. We know how flawed we are, how far we have to grow to become more than just the worst sides of ourselves, but we're willing to make that journey. People like George and Lillian, Four and Envy, were willing to take the shortcuts at the expense of others to attain their goals. We end that tonight."

"Fuck yeah," Sam growled from under his hood somewhere to my left, ruining the pretentious ceremony in a way that was so true to our brotherhood. It had us all chuckling shortly before he sobered again.

"If The Elite is for life, we must either end The Elite or end ourselves. Most of them are gone, dead, or, in George's case, moved into Baton Rouge's premier mental asylum. If anyone remains after tonight to try to pick up the broken thread of the society, let's send a message that we'll be there to fucking beat them back."

My brothers beat their fists against their chests in agreement.

"Follow me," I told them as I turned to walk up the steps into the empty hall of St. Augustine's Cathedral.

Savoie was gone, arrested along with my father and a few others for prostitution, underage pornography, grooming, and a litany of other charges. The cathedral was closed and empty until such a time when the pope could appointment a new archbishop.

Our footsteps echoed over the flagstones as I led them to the confessional on the left side of the pews.

I picked up the gasoline waiting there and tucked it under my arm so I could light the first match.

"Pride," I said, then paused as Mason moved forward. "The Elite has wronged you. They blackmailed you, had you stabbed and beaten in jail where you spent five un-warranted years, and kept you from your sister."

He took the match from me and stepped closer, toss-ing the flaming stick into the slates in the wooden door of the confessional where it fell to the ground and flickered dully.

"Do you pledge to end The Elite and stay loyal to

your own brotherhood, *this brotherhood*, until the end?" I asked him solemnly.

"Fuck yeah."

He stepped back into the semi-circle, and I called Rhett forward, listing the crimes against him and his before handing him the match to throw into the confessional. One by one, my brothers added their kindling to the flames building inside the wooden box until I reached the very end.

"Wrath," I said to Sam, who stepped forward, the shadows catching his hard features in a way that made him look like a demon straight from hell. "The society has wronged you and so has our brotherhood. They raped your woman and took your sister away from you."

I handed him the lit match, then the container of gasoline.

"Do you pledge to end The Elite and stay loyal to your brothers of *this* brotherhood here with you tonight until the end?" I asked him.

"Until the end," he answered.

"Then, let's remind the last betrayer that no one fucks with our brotherhood or our lives," I said as I stepped back to throw open the door of the confessional.

It burst open, flames licking up the door and walls from the fiery floor where two bare feet burned in the heat.

"Burn the envious betrayer," I told Sam, echoing the words of Four with Lillian, giving him permission as Wrath from The Elite and as Sam from his new brotherhood to kill the man who had ruined the lives of his women.

Sam surged forward so quickly, he was a black smear.

The force of the movement and the smoke starting to billow around us threw the hood back from his face. He stared at Envy, at Sebastian Westbrook, as he sat bound and gagged in the flaming confessional.

"You deserve to die a million-fucking times for what you did to Patience and Sab," he ground out, tears and rage tight in his throat. "But I'll be happy to claim the one death as mine."

He uncapped the gasoline, lifted it high over his head, then tipped the entire contents over Envy's prone body. Instantly, the flames leapt higher, eating at the bottom of the walls and licking at Sebastian's booted feet.

Sam watched with the fire dancing light and shadows across his face, grim satisfaction on his lips. We all stepped forward, and I lit the final match as he closed in around the burning man.

"For you," God said, throwing back his hood to speak the rites to me. "You've been wronged by The Elite. They killed your mother and beat your woman."

"They did," I interrupted him. "But I got my vengeance on Savoie and my father. This last match isn't for me..."

I waited a beat, my ears straining to hear the faint thud of feet crossing the marble floors toward us.

A moment later, another figure emerged from the dark, only this time, they were gilded in the gold of the flames.

"It should be Sabella who throws the last match," I said as the fire light lit her up like a phoenix risen from the ashes.

Everyone froze, then turned as one to watch the girl we'd all believed was dead walk forward with her head held high. I could sense Sam was a second away from taking her into his arms and never letting her go, so I stepped beside him and grabbed his arm.

"Let her have this," I whispered.

Sam hesitated, his arm like stone beneath my fingers, before he nodded tersely.

The brothers froze when Micah removed himself from our circle to go to Sabella and take her hand in his. It could have been an offer of assistance, but although Sab looked like she'd been through the ringer, she had no notable injuries.

Yet Sabella accepted Micah's help without hesitation.

I handed her the match when she stopped beside me, but she shook her head.

"We don't have much time, and I want him to confess his sins before he goes to hell," she growled softy, the depth of her rage glittering in her fire bright eyes.

Instantly, Sam stepped forward, lunged through the flames, and ripped the gag from Sebastian's mouth.

The man moaned and screamed wildly until Mason barked, "Shut the fuck up."

Sebastian's pained-filled, drug-glazed eyes rolled in his head, then focused with a snap on Sabella.

"Sab," he whispered through chapped lips. "You didn't leave me. You came back to be my girl."

"Fucking psycho," Rhett spat out.

"Why did you do this to me, you fucking bastard?" she asked him with quiet strength. "Have you done this to women before?"

"One burned," he said, then screamed as the flames started up his calves. "One burned because I wanted her and I had to beat the bastard to get her."

"Karma's a fucking bitch, isn't it?" Sabella taunted, stepping so close to the flaming box that Micah dragged her back a foot so she wouldn't get burned.

I didn't think she would have felt it even if she was consumed by the fire, she was already so mired in the heat of her righteous fury.

Sam lurched forward to grab her, muttering, "Get her the fuck away from that fucker."

God threw an arm around his shoulders, both to comfort him and hold him back, whispering something that seemed to calm him.

"Why me?" Sab demanded over his sobbing cries.

"You were perfect for me," he wailed, tossing his sweat-soaked head back and forth, whimpering from the pain. "You were perfect, and you just couldn't *see* it, so I had to show you."

"By trying to rape me? By taking a knife to my body when I wouldn't let you take your cock to it?" Sabella snarled, tossing her hair back like a cornered stallion ready to bolt forward and trample anything in its path. "You think I was perfect enough to deserve that?"

"It's her fault, her fault, her fault," he said, his broken mind fractured further by the flames. "I thought I tricked her, but she knew I killed him."

"Who?" Sabella ordered.

"Oily Olly! She knew I killed him to be Envy and she made me do so many things…" he slumped forward for a long moment and I thought he'd finally passed out, but then he snapped straight and shouted. "She made me leave Patience, she made me go back to you, then you wanted to leave me. You couldn't go. I couldn't let you go."

We all knew without clarification that he was talking about Lillian.

"I'd bring her back from the fucking dead just to watch her die all over again if I could," Mason muttered darkly.

"You're right. You couldn't let me go. I came back even after you threw me in a swamp to die. I'm stronger than you, Envy. I'm better than you. It's laughable that you ever thought you could make me stay, let alone that you actually deserved me. And now, it's you who has to go," Sab said, then she turned to me and grabbed the box of matches in my hand.

We all watched as she lit one then tossed it into the fire, then another, and another, and onwards, until we were forced to step back because the fire had totally consumed the confessional and was racing up the boards into the rafters to set the entire fucking place on fire.

Finally, Sabella lit the last two matches and walked over to Sam. Wordlessly, they stared at each other for a long moment, the heat in the air waving over them like warped glass.

She handed the last match to her twin brother, and together, they tossed them into the inferno.

Pop! Pop! Pop! Pop! Pop!

The flames had reached the wall behind what was once the confessional, blowing out two of the stained-glass windows.

"Fuck," Mason cursed.

"Holy shit," Rhett hissed.

He was right. The entire holy building was on fire and burning down around our ears. We stared at the burgeoning destruction for one long minute, each of us knowing we had cemented ourselves as sinners of the highest order, no matter the justification of our cause.

Behind us, something burning fell from the sky and crashed into the pews, narrowly missing God. Mason pulled him out of the way, but still, we stood, watching the destruction and listening to the increasing wail of screams and shouts echoing through the hall.

None of us moved to put the fire out or pull Envy from the flames.

We had no doubts. No regrets.

It had to burn.

The church, the society, the traitor among us.

It all had to be razed to the ground.

As one, we turned our backs and ran through the smoke out of the cathedral, down the steps, and onto the grassy slope beneath it.

Our girls were there, waiting in a line to receive us. They would take us home when the time came, make us whole again and show us how to be better people after we'd hit the rock bottom of our dark souls.

But for the moment, everyone waited as I used another canister of gasoline to write three words in the grass.

Sirens wailed in the distance, drawing closer.

The screams from inside faded, then stopped abruptly.

I stepped back, and Rhett, God, and Micah stepped forward to touch their lighters to the words. Sam and Sabella were knotted together like one soul watching on.

We had one last message for The Elite, if any of them remained, and we lit it up with fire before we left the scene of our crime for good.

Brothers over sin.

The message was clear:

No. One. Fucks. With. My. Brothers.

VII

UINCENDUM NATUS

EPILOGUE

Two months later.

"**W**ork for it," I gritted out between clenched teeth. "Ride that cock and show me how much you love having me inside you."

Isabelle threw her head back, her long hair tickling my balls and her ribbon-tied throat exposed as she rode me harder. I loved looking at the ribbon necklace, knowing I had put it there and it denoted my possession over her.

I felt the same way about the tattoo curving around the left side of my ribs that said *lassiez les bons temps rouler*, even though it hurt like a bitch and both Mason and Sam had made fun of me for being such a wimp about it. It was my way to represent my girl and the goodness she had brought into my life. She had changed my life in a permanent way, and I wanted it just as permanent on my skin.

I reached for that ribboned throat and wrapped my hand around just to feel her moans move to her lips and her pulse jump against my thumb. With my other hand, I pulled at her sweet, red nipples until she gasped.

Her movements stuttered as she adjusted to the new, overwhelming sensation, then revved higher, harder. I had her hands tied behind her back with another ribbon so she was working diligently to fuck me with just the power of her slim thighs and plump ass.

"I don't think you're working hard enough, darlin'," I drawled, as if every drag of my cock in and out of her clenching heat wasn't exquisite agony.

I took my hands from her and clasped them behind my head.

"You have one minute to cum before I flip you over and take you there myself," I said, watching as her eyes drifted dazedly along the length of my contracted abs, then flared to mine at the idea I'd planted in her mind. "Put on a show for me. I want to see how bad my good little church mouse can be."

Challenge blazed in her eyes and she licked her kiss-swollen lips before talking in a throaty purr I'd never heard from her before that made my cock throb. "You want me to play with my clit while I ride your big cock?"

"I want you to come all over it," I dared, tilting my hips up hard into her gyrating thrust. "I want your cum dripping down my balls."

I thought she would go quiet. She'd come a long way from the virginal schoolgirl and there was a darkness at the soul of her, a tantalizing deviancy that pulsed between her legs, but occasionally, it still made her feel ashamed.

She surprised me, leaning forward to plant a hand

around *my* throat while the other pressed hard circles over her clit.

Her hot breath tickled my ear as she breathily said, "I love the feel of you stretching my tight pussy. I could ride you like this for hours just using you to get off again and again and…"

Her legs tightened like a vice around my hips, and she reared back, hair flying like a glorious golden-brown flag raised in surrender as she gave into her orgasm and came all over my cock.

"Fuck," I ground out, my hands snapping to her hips to grind her spasming cunt harder against me, my torso knifing up so I could take one of her bouncing breasts in my mouth to suck.

"Come for me, Rush," she moaned. "I want to feel you come inside me."

Her words shot through me like a surge of adrenaline. My muscles locked, the base of my spine clenched, and my balls drew up so painfully, I thought, for one brief second, I would die, and then I came.

Each time with Isabelle was like a religious experience. I felt replete, cleansed, and whole in the way a monk might after days of intense meditation. My entire body sung as we both collapsed, her sweaty body pressed flush to the lines of mine as I wrapped my arms around her and held her close.

"I never thought sex could be like this," Isabelle whispered as she drew lazy circles over my chest with her finger.

"That's because you'd never had sex, let alone with me," I teased.

"No," she said somberly, tilting her chin up to look me

in the eye. "It's because I never knew you could find something so divine outside of a church."

"Darlin'," I murmured, stroking her damp hair away from her flushed face because I didn't know how to transcribe the tenderness in my chest into words.

"It's true, Rush. My entire world view was so narrow because that was the way my father wanted it to be. I never asked questions; I just obeyed. It scares me to think of what my life might have continued to be like if you hadn't interrupted it. It would have been no life at all," she whispered.

"It was fate," I told her. "I was always going to happen to you."

She smiled. "Rush Dempsey doesn't believe in fate or karma or a higher being."

I shrugged. "I'm no longer the guy who gives zero fucks about anything. I care about you, I care about my brothers and their girls, about Buford and Harry. All the shit we went through this year, I have to believe it was for a reason or I'll go fucking crazy."

"You did a lot for them, your brothers."

"Nothing they wouldn't have done for me," I retorted, and I meant it.

We'd started out as a crew of self-centered, arrogant pricks with no agendas but our own. Now, I don't think we would ever allow anyone to disband us.

"For a sinner, you're awfully saintly sometimes," Isabelle teased.

"Maybe. I've changed in so many ways because of this shit, but at the end of the day, I'm a sinner, and there is no doubt I will sin again. The difference is, I know you will be there to hold a mirror to the face of my transgressions and force me to grow from them so when faced with a similar decision again, maybe I'll make a better choice."

"Have I mentioned today that I love you?" she asked, awe and joy suffused in her beautiful face.

She'd taken to wearing subtle makeup and nicer clothes, things that flattered her willow form and tantalized me with their feminine sensuality, but I still loved her best barefaced and flushed as she was then staring up at me.

"No, but honest to Christ, I feel it in my chest every day, whether you say so or not."

"Romantic," she accused playfully, softly because she loved it.

"Dirty," I rejoined with a little smack to her ass. "As much as I would love to keep you in this bed all day, you've got an important job to do, and I've got someone important to see."

Immediately, her face flashed red then white and her perfect mouth dropped open. "Oh, my goodness, what time is it?"

I laughed as she jumped off me and flew into the bathroom. "Relax, you've got time."

The shower went on, then she poked her head out of the door to glare at me. "I have to be there *early*, Rush. It's my first day, and I don't have anyone to show me the ropes because the old guidance counselor is *dead*."

I propped some pillows behind my back and leaned over to grab one of my hand-rolled joints from the nightstand. Isabelle was softening on her stance toward marijuana, mostly because she realized I would never stop blazing, and I took full advantage of that.

I lit the weed cigarette and stuck it between my lips before calling out, "Lillian was the shittiest fucking guidance counselor the world has ever seen. You'll be ten times better than her."

"I haven't even officially graduated yet," she cried out from the other room. "You and God shouldn't have pulled strings to get me the interim position."

I didn't tell her it wasn't actually temporary, that she'd have the job for as long as she fucking well wanted it. She was qualified; a Master's in behavioral psychology was more than Lillian fucking Griffin had ever had, but we'd had our first fight after I told her she got the position without even applying.

I didn't give a fuck. She needed a job, she would kick ass at it, and we needed someone we trusted in a position of influence at St. Augustine.

"You're the opposite of Lillian," I said instead, reluctantly getting out of bed to get dressed for my own work of the day. "You're goodness personified whereas she was everything evil. It's an automatic upgrade for the kids who need guidance and advice at this time in their lives."

Isabelle peeked around the doorframe again, this time her face gentle in a way that made my heart clench. "Well then, I guess if my normally faithless boyfriend believes in me, I can totally do the job."

I winked at her. "That's my girl. I'll be gone when you get out of the shower, but I'll see you later when you get home."

"Yeah," she said even softer, her eyes velvet with warmth. "See you at home later, honey."

I smiled as she ducked back into the bathroom, then I whistled as I got dressed. The Dempsey compound had never felt like home, not even when my mother was alive. The home I'd bought as an escape as soon as I hit eighteen was now exactly like a real-life dream house, the kind my father had always alluded to having but never actually sought.

I had a home and a woman I would die for.

There was nothing dreamier than that.

And for the first time in my life, my restless, bored soul was finally at fucking peace.

Isabelle

The office was stripped to the studs. There wasn't even a desk in the vacant room, just a few boxes of documents and an unplugged Mac desktop pushed to one side of the room. It was inconvenient, but I was glad. I didn't want any trace of Lillian Griffin and her poisonous energy left in the space that would now be mine.

Mine.

Isabelle Savoie, St. Augustine's guidance counselor.

The reward of that title rolled through me like a gentle spring rain, cleansing my soul of the last vestiges of darkness and insecurity that lingered there.

I was a new kind of woman, one with an important job and a serious, adult relationship. I had friends for the first time in my life, women who cared about me just as much as I cared about them. I had the time and inclination to pursue things I'd never been given reign to explore. I'd joined a knitting club to indulge my passion, a kickboxing club with Sabella to learn how to defend myself, and together with Z, we were working to overhaul the orphanage that had been corrupted for so long.

I was whole and dynamic, a woman of multitudes just as women naturally would be if they were not repressed by men.

The feeling of walking into the office knowing it was mine and I deserved it defied description.

But I imagined it felt very much like being ordained over years of worship.

I'd earned this.

Not just through my diligent studies, but because I'd been through hell and emerged even stronger than before.

I touched my fingers to the top box, then pulled off the lid to see what I had to deal with before I got down to ordering furniture.

My hand flew up to cover my mouth when I saw what was inside.

A glass and chrome nameplate that read: Isabelle Savoie. Guidance Counselor.

Tied to it with a red ribbon was a small note decorated with Rush's small block script that read:

CHURCH MOUSE,

I WOULD HAND YOU THE WORLD IF I THOUGHT IT WOULD BRING A SMILE TO MY GIRL'S FACE, BUT I THOUGHT THIS WAS A GOOD PLACE TO START. NO ONE WILL EVER BE PROUDER OR MORE IN LOVE WITH YOU THAN I AM. YOU MAKE ME BELIEVE IN THE GOODNESS OF THE WORLD AND I KNOW THESE STUDENTS WILL BENEFIT FROM YOUR LIGHT JUST AS MUCH AS I HAVE.

LOVE,
YOUR WICKED HOT BOYFRIEND

I sobbed against my hand as I read the note, then jumped when a voice sounded behind me.

"Chas you owe me ten bucks," Megan said as I spun around to face her and the rest of the holy virtue women walking through the door.

Chastity scoffed. "I didn't take you up on the bet. We all knew she'd cry at some point today."

"Hey," I protested through my tears, crying even harder now because my girlfriends had come to help me settle in on my first day and it felt so good to know I had friends like that. "I'm not a crybaby!"

"No," Z agreed, moving forward with a beaming smile to grab my hands and give them a squeeze. "But you did cry when I told you God and I got married."

"That's a big deal!" I protested, then looked over her shoulder at the other girls. "Didn't you guys cry?"

No one answered for a moment, then Patience bit her lip, and said, "I think I might have teared up?"

I blinked at her, then burst out laughing. I'd been doing that a lot since Rush and the girls came into my life, but it still felt precious and delicious each time it happened.

"Okay, so I'm a crybaby," I admitted. "I can live with that. Happy things in life should be celebrated, especially after everything we've been through."

"Amen to that," Chastity agreed. "Which is exactly why we came to take you out for a celebratory lunch to commune about our guys and your new job!"

"It's not even noon yet," I told them. "I just got here and I have so much to do…"

Megan rolled her eyes. "You need to order furniture before you do anything else, and we can do that on my phone while sipping mimosas at Sneaky Pickle."

"Before you say no," Patience jumped in, "we will be working, in a sense. We've been thinking about what you said, and we're all down to help you."

"With what?" I asked blankly.

Sabella righted herself from the doorway she'd been leaning against, flipping her switch blade open and closed. "Starting a charity for abused women. I know it was probably an off-hand comment, but God told Z he would give us the start-up money and we want to do it. All of us."

"Who better to found something like that then the six of us?" Patience asked, a bitter sadness to her voice.

It was true. I had suggested the idea in passing, thinking it would be a good project for the future. I didn't have the time to start something like that by myself, but with the help of the girls, it would not only be possible but incredibly healing. We needed it as much as those women of abuse needed us.

The emptiness I'd felt in my gut now that I wasn't involved in the church, helping people find their paths through God, suddenly filled up inside my soul. I didn't need the parameters of religion to do good. I could do it just because I was good and I wanted to do right by the world.

I gazed around the empty room I intended to fill with eager kids and tools to help them find their way in life and sighed before nodding my head.

"Fine, but first order of business is buying me a desk."

"Done," Megan said with a little dance. "Now, let's get those mimosas."

"One more thing," I said, linking my hand with Z's, then pulling in Patience with my othe,. "I think we should use a play on the holy virtues for the name. I was thinking Virtue of Safety Women's Aid."

Sabella's normally hard face softened slightly as she stared at me for a long moment. When she walked across the floor to me, I was momentarily scared of her. She had been through a lot, and sometimes, there was so much darkness in her gaze, I wasn't sure she'd ever function without wrath again.

She placed a hand on my shoulder and squeezed gently before giving me a small smile. "I love it. It's perfect."

Megan ruined our moment by crying out, "Great! Done. Virtue of Safety's first meeting is down the road at Sneaky Pickle. We can toast over those mimosas."

We all laughed as we filtered out the door. I couldn't remember if I'd ever had a better day than I was having then, waking up beside the love of my life and walking between women I'd go to the ends of the earth for. I thought about the song Rush had played for me the first night we spent together, how it spoke of searching for something to fulfill you.

And I realized with sudden brilliant and tender shock, I had found that something, against all odds, at St. Augustine, with a sinner and a group of broken saints.

Rush

The rally was inside one of New Orleans Airport's empty airplane hangars, the massive space filled with supporters and media, cameras and hand-written signs of support partially obscuring the bottom of the platform where the popular candidate stood, giving his speech.

He was a fantastic orator, his voice carved out the words in clean, smooth lines that seemed to present his philosophies as statutes of ancient wisdom. I noticed the flush in women's cheeks as they stared at him, aroused by his good looks and passion, and the self-satisfied smiles of men who believed he spoke for them.

The VP himself had flown out to endorse his run for senate.

Malcom Benedict was going to win the race by a fucking landslide.

I knew the ins and outs of politics the way Isabelle knew religion. I'd grown up with it, been breastfeed on it. I knew the signs of success and the smell of change in the air.

Now that Ward was out of the picture—currently living out a twenty-year sentence in a beautiful white-collar prison in Shreveport—it was all Malcom's for the taking.

One of my brothers, Levi, had even jumped ship to work for his campaign.

I'd been justifiably nervous meeting with my three older brothers for the first time after dad was incarcerated, largely because of *me*.

I shouldn't have been.

Unbeknownst to me, they hated Ward just as much as I did. They just hid it better, used our father for his connections and otherwise ignored him and New Orleans to carve out their own futures.

They were more than willing to work together with the new Elite to make a change. One of those changes was to install Levi in Malcom's camp to keep an eye on the bastard. We'd laughed when Benedict had taken him on with a smug smile like the cat that ate the fucking canary.

Having a Dempsey in his camp was the ultimate defeat of his rival.

It was also the installation of a pawn we needed to ensure the eventual defeat of ours; him.

I waited by the left side of the stage throughout the address, my hands in my pockets and my shoulders slouched. I was dressed mutedly in a pale blue button-up and dark jeans, my bright gold hair hidden under a navy blue ball-cap.

Malcom still sensed me the moment I stationed myself there, his predator's instincts identifying a threat on his territory.

He stared at me as he spoke about bettering the state of Louisiana, "Trust in me as your higher power to get the things that need to be done finished before it's too late."

I snorted softly, but maintained eye contact with him as I let out a huge yawn.

He didn't look at me again after that.

But I wasn't surprised when an aid shuffled out after the speech to tell me Mr. Benedict wanted to have a word with me in the back room.

God had been to see the asshole a couple weeks ago because he'd been "summoned" to talk about what Malcom could do for his future. He'd basically spit in his face.

So, Malcom was ready for me when I entered the room, fingers steepled, legs crossed and face stapled to a look of contempt.

"Sloth," he began, "it's long past time you brought me the book."

I leaned a shoulder against the doorjamb instead of stepping inside to close the door behind me. "I'm surprised you need it. There's nothing incriminating about you in it, which is in itself curious because there is something incriminating about *everyone* in The Elite in that thing."

"You speak about it as if you don't have it with you," Malcom surmised with narrowed eyes. "I expect to receive it."

"I'm sure you do. You seem to expect everything to go your way," I drawled. "Come to think of it, even the mysterious death of Four seems to have been beneficial to you. Now, you don't need to worry about him pitting his money against your influence in a war of wills if you ever disagree."

Malcom stared at me for a long moment before he got up, moved behind me and closed the door. "Sit down, Rush," he demanded, retaking his seat.

I considered his order for long enough to have him glaring at me before I strolled over and flopped into the chair across his desk. "You killed him."

It was the only thing that made sense. God had called me yesterday to tell me his father's autopsy had come back.

Four was poisoned.

"It was clever of you," I continued when Malcom only stared at me in boredom. "No one would suspect the gluttonous, obese bastard would have a heart attack. It was only a matter of time. If God wasn't such a suspicious asshole, there never would have been an autopsy and Four would have been forgotten in the ground."

"If you think I'm as stupid as your father was and I'll

confess so you can record it and send it to the FBI, you can get up and leave right now," Malcom said, completely unflappable.

I dug my phone out of my pocket and tossed it onto the desk. "Check it. Nothing there. I doubt I'd be able to incriminate you even if you did confess. You are The Elite. Is there anything you can't get out of?"

My compliment to his pride had him smiling thinly. "No, I don't imagine there is. That was something Ward and Four didn't seem to understand."

"So you had them taken care of," I concluded. "You used Ward's own son against him and poisoned the glutton. So poetic."

Malcom opened his hands wide in a gesture of humble agreement. "I can't take credit for the actual poisoning. I think you can understand more than most I'm not a man who does things if someone else can do them for him."

My stomach turned sour at the comparison. He'd made many in my company, alluding to the fact that we were similar somehow, that I could be him if I only allowed myself.

I wouldn't and couldn't be.

Not with my brothers to support me and my woman to check my morality.

But maybe, in another life…and that was enough to make me sick.

"Who did it?" I asked.

"Your brother was supposed to," he admitted as if I should know, side eyeing me to check my reaction. "But like the rest of you, he proved a disappointment."

My mind raced thinking about who he could have tasked with killing Four.

God was out, obviously, and Rhett with him because he was too loyal to his best friend. Envy was Lillian's puppet and even the bitch had been frightened of Malcom so that was a possibility, but something in my gut told me it was someone else.

"All this for a place on the senate?" I asked, putting my thoughts on the back burner for later.

I was there for reconnaissance. Malcom seemed to view me with more respect than the rest and I intended to take advantage of it. He was the last vestige of the old guard and we needed all the help we could get to take him down.

"All this for unlimited power, Rush. Don't be so small minded," Malcom chided. "You see, The Elite is mine now. With Four, George, Ward, and Lillian gone, there is no one else to get in my way of using the society the way it always should have be used, for the assumption of power."

"Power not for just one man," I reminded him through gritted teeth. "The Elite was always meant to be about brotherhood above all else."

"Tell yourself that fairytale if it helps you sleep at night, but I think we both know better. You can judge me all you want, Rush. Even knowing who I was in the organization, you took information from me to take your father down. You used ill-gotten gains to succeed at a game you wanted to win at all costs. Will you really try to blame me for doing the same?"

"It's completely different," I argued.

He raised a brow. "Is it? You don't know my story. Maybe I was abused or assaulted, manipulated and deceived as a child and I'm only looking for my just desserts."

"Were you?" I asked, my voice weighted with cynicism.

Cruel delight danced in his pale blue eyes. "No."

"I'm not giving you the book," I told him, standing up to place my palms on his desk and leaning forward into his space. "I'm not giving you anything else in your selfish crusade. You won't be able to use me or my brothers again."

"Won't I?" he asked with glittering eyes. "I think I've proven time and time again you don't have a say in the matter. How do you know I'm not using you right now? That I didn't plan for exactly this?"

I didn't, and a deep shiver ripped like a broken zipper up my back. "It might not be today or tomorrow or even fucking ten years from now, but we're going to take you down and fucking bury you alive in a way that you'll never be able to breathe free again."

"You can try," Malcom invited with a dark chuckle. "I might even enjoy watching that."

"Then game fucking on," I decreed as I grabbed my phone from the desk and turned on my heel to leave.

"Game on," Malcom said quietly from behind me as I opened the door and moved into the hall. "May the worst man win."

I kept my pace steady as I moved down the back hall, through the empty front room before the stage, and outside into the wet New Orleans summer heat. Only when I was safely ensconced in the Rolls and Buford was pulling out from the parking lot did I look at my phone.

Me: Did you get it?

I waited, drumming my fingers against my thigh. I'd worked for months on the project, long before I had anything to test it on. It was what I'd worked on at night when I couldn't sleep, in the middle of class when the professors failed to hold my attention. It was the tech that would make my career if it was successful.

The tech that would change the game I'd just willingly entered into.

Harriet: Got it.

I fist-pumped silently, then shot off a text to the only man who hated Malcom Benedict more than me.

Me: We got it. Tag, Micah, you're it."

VII

UINCENDUM NATUS

EXTENDED EPILOGUE

Rush

One month later.

I t was time. After over a year of turmoil and agony, the
time had come for us to take down the final player on
the board of The Elite. He was in checkmate, standing
alone across the room surrounded by his enemies with no
recourse but to get on his knees and fucking beg for our
mercy.

We would grant none.

This was the moment we had been waiting for. We
wanted to relish in it, fucking gorge ourselves on it. Beside
me, Rhett practically vibrated with suppressed energy,
and on his other side, Sam growled subconsciously.

We could smell the blood in the water.

Malcom was ours.

Bang!

The sharp sound reverberated throughout the room, throwing everything into chaos.

There was blood—so much blood—and the agonizing shouts of more than one man.

I collapsed to my knees and crawled across the floor, my heart a dead weight in my chest as I whispered, "Fuck no. Fuck no."

This wasn't how it was supposed to go. This wasn't the ending we'd sought.

We meant it to end with a whimper.

Instead, it ended with a bang.

The End... for now...

PLAYLIST

"Seven Devils" — Florence + The Machine

"Waiting Game" — BANKS

"Teen Idle" — MARINA

"Sweet Dreams" — Emily Browning

"Me and The Devil" —Soap&Skin

"Hallelujah" — Jeff Buckley

"Everybody Wants To Rule The World" — Lorde

"Control" — Halsey

"Glory And Gore" — Lorde

"If I Had A Heart" — Fever Ray

"Special Death" — Mirah

"Eyes On Fire" — Blue Foundation

Listen now on Spotify!

ACKNOWLEDGMENTS

When Ker Dukey and K Webster approached me about writing a project about a secret society based on the Seven Deadly Sins, I was hooked immediately. It was such an amazing concept and an opportunity to work with a wonderful group of authors and women who I grew to deeply admired. I landed with the sin of Sloth, which is ironic, because anyone that knows me knows that I am a bundle of energy with millions of things on the go at the same time. At first, I struggled with how to make a character that was supposed to resemble Sloth sexy. Then I saw a picture on Pinterest of a handsome young man standing in an apathetic slouch with his head thrown back and slightly to his side as if he gave zero fucks about anything around him. Instantly, Rush Dempsey unveiled himself in my mind as an entitled, lazy boy with no drive who is turned on his head when his beloved mother dies and turns into one of the masterminds of the whole series. Sloth also means apathy toward religion, which is why his task was linked to the church and his heart became linked to his 'church mouse.' As in the other books in the series, my hero and heroine are foils of each other that bring out the best in the other person and I loved creating Isabelle to be a good, pious little virgin who begins learns that not everything is black and white.

Thank you so much to Ker Dukey for taking on the strain of being our Pride and leader for this project. You carried this universe on your shoulders like motherfucking Atlas and I'm so proud of you for your grace and strength and grateful to you for allowing me to be a part of this project.

K, I love your form of krazy. Thank you for thinking of me for this project, but more, thank you for being such a daddy-loving, taboo creating friend to me. You're an inspiration and constant support.

To the other ladies—Jessica, Missy, and Claire— it was a delight to work with you talented authors and wonderful humans.

To Serena, who always gets a massive thanks in my acknowledgements because my ship would be rudderless without her, thank you for all the things. You're the sweet friend, the best PA, and a truly amazing woman. Oh, and thanks for coining Rush's term 'zero fucks to give!'

Allaa, I don't even know how to properly express all the ways you provide kindling for my creative spirit and gentle guidance when I let my creative A.D.D. get the best of me. You're a pillar of my writing world and I'm so lucky to have you.

Sarah, you are the best beta reader an author could ever have. Seriously, I know I'm a mess and you always find all the ways I need to tidy my shit up. Thank you and please, never leave me.

Michelle, my soul sister, I love you and your love buoys me through all my bad times, book related or not.

Ella, I just love you. That's all and that's everything.

Stacey at Champagne Formatting is a genius and a wizard. Thank you for making my books so pretty and doing it so quickly on my tight schedule all the time. You rock.

Monica from Nerd Word Editing, thank you for being such a champion editing this series. I know I didn't make it easy for you with Sloth, but you have my endless respect and gratitude for working with me on it.

Giana's Darlings, you are the best reader's group on the planet and my safe, little happy place on the interweb. I love talking with you all about books, boys, and real-life problems. It's like having my own personal girl squad and that's pretty freaking cool.

To all the bloggers, instagrammers, and readers who took the time to anticipate, read, and review this series, I cannot tell you how much it means to me and my fellow authors. We poured so much time and energy into this series and the ultimate validation is always your love for our words. So, thank you from the bottom of my heart for your enthusiasm for The Elite!

To my sister Grace who demands the next book on my schedule before I've even written a word of it. You've also been a staunch support of my writing and it means everything to me.

To my Armie. Couldn't live this life without you and wouldn't want to. In all my years of reading about best friends, I never truly understood the meaning of endless platonic love until I met you.

As always, last, but never least, to the LOML. Thank you for being patient with me when I'm an hour late to hang out because I got caught up writing, for supporting my mood swings when I'm stressed about a plot point or deadline and for knowing that chocolate will always perk me up. This book is about faith in so many ways and you've always had faith in me and in us, even when I didn't. Your strength is my light in the dark and I'm so grateful for it.

ABOUT THE AUTHOR

Giana Darling is a Top 40 Best Selling Canadian romance writer who specializes in the taboo and angsty side of love and romance. She currently lives in beautiful British Columbia where she spends time riding on the back of her man's bike, baking pies, and reading snuggled up with her cat Persephone.

OTHER BOOKS BY GIANA

THE EVOLUTION OF SIN TRILOGY:
The Affair (The Evolution of Sin #1)
The Secret (The Evolution of Sin #2)
The Consequence (The Evolution of Sin #3)
The Evolution of Sin Trilogy Boxset

THE ENSLAVED DUET
Enthralled (The Enslaved Duet, Book 1)
Enamoured (The Enslaved Duet, Book 2)

THE FALLEN MEN SERIES:
Lessons in Corruption (The Fallen Men Series #1)
Welcome to the Dark Side (The Fallen Men Series #2)
Good Gone Bad (The Fallen Men Series #3)

COMING SOON:
After the Fall (The Fallen Men Series #4)

Join my Reader's Group:
www.facebook.com/groups/819875051521137

Follow me on Twitter:
www.twitter.com/GianaDarling

Like me on Facebook:
www.facebook.com/gianadarling

Subscribe to my blog:
gianadarling.com

Follow me on Pinterest:
www.pinterest.com/gianadarling

Follow me on Goodreads:
www.goodreads.com/author/show/14901102.Giana_Darling

Newsletter:
eepurl.com/b0qnPr

IG:
www.instagram.com/gianadarlingauthor